BY
POPULAR
DEMAND

ALSO BY JESS VALLANCE

Featuring Gracie Dart:
You Only Live Once
To Be Perfectly Honest

The Yellow Room
Birdy

Jess Vallance

BY
POPULAR
DEMAND

HOT
KEY
BOOKS

First published in Great Britain in 2019 by
HOT KEY BOOKS
80–81 Wimpole St, London W1G 9RE
www.hotkeybooks.com

This is a work of fiction. Names, places, events and incidents are either
the products of the author's imagination or used fictitiously. Any
resemblance to actual persons, living or dead, is purely coincidental.

A CIP catalogue record for this book is available from the British Library.

ISBN: 9781471407703
also available as an ebook

1

This book is typeset using Atomik ePublisher
Printed and bound in Great Britain by Clays Ltd, Elcograf S.p.A.

Hot Key Books is an imprint of Bonnier Books UK
www.bonnierbooks.co.uk

PART 1:

Where I contemplate a future with only a pie for company

Hoe-down

It was Saturday night and I was having a perfectly sophisticated evening in with my two good friends, Til and Reeta. We were in my bedroom watching a critically acclaimed French film set in picturesque Provence. I had laid on an elegant buffet of culinary delights, inspired by cuisines from around the world.

'Why is it all so small?' Til said, picking up a bite-size feta-and-tomato tart. 'It makes me feel like a giant, holding this fiddly little stuff in my big hands.'

'That's how it's supposed to be,' I explained. 'They're appetizers. *Hors d'oeuvres.*'

Til looked at me, then down at the snacks, then at me again. Her face was blank.

I sighed. 'It's not meant to be *dinner*. I never said I was making you dinner. They're just to taste. They're *amuse-bouches*. They're meant to amuse your *bouche*.'

Til frowned, pushed the tiny tart into her mouth and chewed thoughtfully.

'Why have you put the grapes on sticks though?' Reeta asked, picking up a cocktail stick and twirling it around.

'They're not grapes,' I told her. 'They're olives.'

Reeta put one in her mouth, but after just one chew her eyes widened and she spat it back into her hand. 'I think they're off, Gracie,' she said, wiping her mouth with the back of her hand.

'They're not off, I only got them today.' I put one in my mouth. 'See,' I said, chewing the salty ball. 'They're fine. They're . . . delicious.' I forced myself to swallow.

Reeta tipped the mangled remains of hers into a plant pot in the corner of my room. 'Sorry,' she said, shaking her head sadly. 'I think my tongue is allergic to them.' She reached into her bag and took out a pint-size carton of milk and drank it down in one go.

'They're just an acquired taste,' I said, taking another olive from the plate. 'If you don't get through the barrier, you'll never acquire it.'

Til frowned. 'As in, no pain, no gain?'

I nodded. 'Exactly. We're in college now, for heaven's sake. We need to make an effort to mature. Do you want to be the only adults in history to still be eating Cheestrings and boxes of raisins like a baby? Because I do not.'

Til peered at the olives again, but decided against taking one. She leant against the end of my bed and turned back to the television.

Although the film was very interesting and packed full of beautiful fields of wild flowers and farmers having lively conversations in the middle of those fields, I was checking my phone regularly. Every thirty seconds, to be precise. This wasn't because I was bored, you understand, but just in case some very serious news should break that I would need to report to the others.

As I scrolled through with one eye on the TV, where a French farmer was shouting angrily at the sky, I noticed that a lot of the photos in my feed seemed to have been taken in the same place: some kind of American diner. It had a bar lined with neon-pink lights and posters from classic films all over the walls.

Lots of the photos showed people from college standing behind the bar, spooning ice cream into blenders or stirring big glasses with stripy straws. Everyone seemed to be wearing strange clothes. Ellie from my business studies class was wearing what looked like a cheerleader's dress, with a set of pompoms slung over her shoulder. Jonathan Jones – or Jon-Jon as everyone called him – was dressed as a cowboy, and Martin had, for some reason, wrapped himself in a sheet, put on a spiky cardboard hat and painted his face grey.

'Is *every*one from college in a diner tonight or what?' I passed my phone to Til and she squinted at the screen. 'And what are they all wearing? "American Dream", they're all saying. "Hashtag American Dream". What are they *doing*?'

'It's for Jon-Jon's birthday,' Til said, passing my phone back to me. 'It's an American party in that new diner by the pier.'

New photos were appearing every few minutes or so. In the latest batch, Martin seemed to be holding his sheet-skirts up around his knees and tap dancing. 'Why has Martin come as a Roman?'

Til shrugged. 'They're doing a milkshake workshop first. Then later there's going to be music and that. Jon-Jon's got the whole place hired until eleven. Should be a cool night.'

I sighed. 'Why do *we* never get invited? Why do we never get invited to cool nights?'

Til didn't reply, which wasn't unusual, but Reeta was staring hard at the television, her mouth clamped shut like she was afraid some words might escape if she didn't very consciously hold them in. She wasn't even blinking.

'Reeta . . . ?'

'Nope!' she said, in a too-loud voice, her eyes still fixed on the screen. 'No! Nothing!'

I frowned. 'What's nothing?'

She looked at me then, her eyes wide. 'I don't know! Nothing!'

I peered at her. 'You were invited, weren't you? To Jon-Jon's American hoe-down milk-fest diner-thon?'

Reeta still didn't say anything. She just turned to look at Til, who shifted uncomfortably on her bean-bag.

'You as well!' I threw an olive at her.

Til ducked and the olive bounced off the window sill and into my laundry bin. 'Sorry, man. But, I thought you didn't like Jon-Jon? Remember, you said he always talks like a gameshow host?'

'He does! Everyone says that!'

'Yeah, but you said it *to* him.'

I was quiet. He did talk like that. He would put his arm around your shoulder and lean in far too close and say, 'Hello, Grace, and how are you today, are you having a good day?' And then if you ever tried to reply to him he would get bored immediately and start talking over the top of you. Til was right. I didn't like him. But that was hardly the point.

'That's hardly the point,' I said. 'Loads of people don't like him. You don't like him. But you're invited and I'm not. It's . . . victimisation!'

Til rolled her eyes. 'We're here, aren't we? We're here now, at your French film and amusing-bouche evening, rather than down at the diner?'

'I was just thinking actually . . .' Reeta began quietly and I turned to look at her. She picked up a magazine, rolled it into the shape of a tube, angled it in Til's direction and spoke into it, as if that way I wouldn't hear what she was saying. 'We should . . . go . . . ?'

She looked at Til nervously.

Til frowned. 'Reeta!' she hissed.

I looked between them. 'What? What's this? Where should you go?'

They looked sheepishly at each other, and then down at the ground.

'Oh, right. I get it.' I folded my arms. 'I see what's going on here. You're going, aren't you? That's your real plan for tonight. You just popped in here to keep me quiet – to do your bit and entertain your loser friend for a few hours – but you both can't wait to get out of here and down to the proper party!'

Neither of them said anything.

'Fine,' I said, turning off the TV and tossing the remote

down on the duvet. 'Go. Go on. Go and wrap yourself in a sheet and eat hot dogs made of horse's hooves and wave your stars-and-stripes flags. It's quite clear my efforts at real food and sophisticated entertainment are wasted on you.'

'We do need to get going . . .' Til said quietly.

They both got to their feet and picked up their stuff.

'Sorry, Gracie,' Reeta said, taking her coat down from the hook on the back of my bedroom door. 'Thanks for –'

'Just go!' I said, cutting her off and turning my head away from them as they made their sorry exit.

Once they'd gone, I prepared myself a small platter of olives, feta tarts and slices of expensive cooked ham. I put the film back on and tried to concentrate on the subtitles as one man in a hat told a man in a different type of hat something very important about the ground.

Obviously, I'd much rather be here, I told myself, with this intelligent film and this elegant finger food. Far better to be indoors, in my own space, enjoying the peace and quiet, than wearing some ridiculous outfit in a sweaty diner with boring idiots like Jon-Jon talking over everyone.

I couldn't stop myself from taking a few sneaky looks at my phone though and it wasn't long before, in the constant stream of photos everyone seemed to feel the need to upload, Til and Reeta appeared. Til was wearing a yellow T-shirt with 'lifeguard' written across the front in big red letters and was carrying a red plastic swimming float. Reeta had handcuffs dangling from one wrist and was wearing a bright orange jumpsuit like a prisoner would wear.

I didn't see what any of it had to do with America. There were lifeguards and prisoners in all countries, weren't there? Really, what was the point in having a theme if no one was even going to stick to it?

My phone flashed. A video upload from Martin. It was of himself, grinning at the camera in his strange sheet costume, holding a cone of chips.

I typed a reply.

Me: Why are you dressed as a Roman emperor?

Martin: Statue of Liberty! Why aren't you here?

Me: Not invited

Martin: Sucks to be you!

I turned the TV off again and shoved the remote under my pillow.

Martin was right. It did.

Sheila Wheeler

I'd started my new job at Podrick's Hardware Store just a few weeks earlier.

It was a little shop down a quiet road on the way to Til's flat that had probably been the same for about a hundred years, and sold everything from sink plugs and hammers to yoga bricks and fairy lights shaped like flamingos. When I'd been unceremoniously sacked from my last job at a steakhouse called the Ranch, my only crime being to offer a regular customer my services as a love-life advisor, I thought I may never work in this town again. But luckily I'd only been unemployed for a few days when Leonard, the owner of Podrick's, agreed to take me on.

The shop was tucked away so it was usually quite quiet and I spent most of my shifts there flicking through a magazine or looking at my phone behind the till, occasionally looking up to ring through a bottle of carpet shampoo or a mousetrap. Once or twice a week a customer would hugely overestimate my knowledge of the products in the shop and how they should be used, and would ask me what kind of fixture they should buy to put up a mirror or what size batteries they needed for a portable disco ball. If I was feeling helpful when they asked, I would look up the answer on my phone but, more often than not, I'd direct them to my colleague, Sheila Wheeler, who had worked at Podrick's for years and years.

Sheila Wheeler may have been eighty years old or may have been forty. There was really no way to know for sure. She had white hair that stuck straight out of her head like a candy-floss hat; she wore a watch around her neck on a chain and kept a cigarette tucked behind her ear at all times. Sheila could tell you not only exactly which product was stored in which section of which shelf in the shop, but she could tell you what used to be shelved there on any given year in the past and exactly when and why it had been replaced. There wasn't a square foot of the shop that Sheila didn't know the entire history of.

'Do you know where the de-icer's kept?' I'd ask, for example.

'Far-left corner, third shelf from the bottom, two blocks in.' But she wouldn't stop there. 'Just above the fingerless gloves. Where we used to keep the candles from 2004 to 2006 and where we used to keep the light-up yo-yos until that little lad swallowed a bulb and the whole lot had to be sent back to the factory.'

I didn't mind Sheila. After my first hour in the shop, she treated me as if I'd worked there my whole life. This did mean that she seemed surprised when I didn't know how to change a till roll or when I didn't realise that the blue neon sign reading FIRE that flashed from time to time just meant that there was a delivery at the back door and not that we needed to evacuate immediately, but it also meant she left me alone. She would tuck herself away in the corner of the shop, sometimes tidying shelves and restacking tea towels, sometimes just doing the crossword on the back of the paper, and I was free to sit behind the counter and mind my own business.

The day after Jon-Jon's American Dream milkshake party that I wasn't invited to, I had a shift at Podrick's starting as usual at 9 a.m. I was still grumpy about being left out and had ignored three messages from Reeta and one from Til.

A man in bright-red trousers and a waistcoat strolled into the shop. He wandered around with his hands in his pockets, whistling like he'd come for a day out rather than to buy anything in particular. He stopped in front of the Bargain Bucket – a wire basket we kept just in front of the till, labelled with a sign saying:

All items £1

'Everything one pound, is it?' he said.

'Yes, that's right,' I said. Then I added, 'Just a pound,' because it felt like I should say more, but there really wasn't anything else to say about it.

He picked up a bottle opener shaped like a garden spade. 'A pound?' he asked.

'Yep,' I said.

'And this?' This time he was holding up a packet of gold pens.

12

'One pound, yes. Everything in there is a pound.'

He nodded and continued to rifle through. Then a smile crept slowly over his face. 'How about,' he said, holding up a can of air freshener in one hand and a packet of radish seeds in the other, 'if I want two things? Bet it's not one pound then, is it?'

I frowned at him. 'That would be two pounds,' I said slowly. 'One pound for each item.'

'Aha!' He threw the things back into the basket. 'I knew it! There is always a trick with these things! That, young lady, is why I always read the small print.'

'OK,' I said, because really, what else was there to say?

With this, he clearly felt his point was made and his use for the shop was exhausted because he strolled out, shaking his head and muttering, 'One pound, my foot.'

When he'd gone, Sheila ambled over to the counter. She unfolded the fraying deck-chair she kept tucked underneath it and sat down heavily. She placed her crossword in her lap and took a pencil out of the pocket of her Podrick's T-shirt.

'He was a plonker, then,' she said, nodding her head in the direction of the door the man had just left through. 'Some people talk to strangers just to hear the sound of their own voice, don't they.'

'Yeah.'

'I myself can't bear it,' she went on, leaning over her crossword with her pencil poised. 'My old dad – dead and gone now, died in '98 – he used to say to us kids that when we're born we only have a certain number of words in us to last a lifetime and that when they were used up, that was it.

13

So we shouldn't prattle on too much because we might find when we're thirty-five we've run out all together and we can never say another word.' She paused while she carefully filled in some of the boxes in her puzzle. 'It worked, I can tell you. We weren't talkers, any of us in our house. We could go a whole weekend and the only words that would break the silence would be "pass the fruitcake" and "has anyone seen my underpants".'

My phone vibrated on the top of the counter. It was another message from Til. I didn't bother opening it.

'I don't know how you bear it,' Sheila said, nodding towards the phone. 'Dreadful things. I would never have one. I haven't even got one in my house, let alone one you have to cart about with you.'

'You haven't even got a house phone?'

She shook her head. 'Nope. Got rid of it in 2005. Had enough of people ringing up, trying to sell me things, night and day.'

'What about if someone wants to talk to you? How do you arrange stuff? What if you want to meet someone? How would you know where to go?'

Sheila laughed loudly like I'd made a great joke. 'Meet who! Why would I want to meet anyone? When I go home from this place of an evening, I close the door and I know I'm not going to see another living person until I come back here. I feel sorry for people whose lives are filled with having to meet people, one after another. Always someone's wedding or tea party or birthday to go to.

'I tell you, for my birthday last year I got one of the good pork pies from Waitrose and a bottle of nice ale and I sat down in front my own telly and I watched the entire final of the 1992 US Open. Sampras and Edberg. An absolute corker of a match. I watch it every year, for my birthday. Just me, the pie, the tennis. No people turning up with their cheap flimsy cards to clutter up the shelves. No dried-up pot plant or itchy pyjamas I have to pretend to like. No sitting around listening to people whinge about their children or their grandchildren or why the gear stick's wobbly on their Ford Focus. Just me, on my tod. And a very happy birthday it was too.

'Because that, I tell you, Grace my girl, is the route to true happiness. Ditch the hangers-on. I can see you're like me at heart, you haven't got time for it all either. It's tough, I know, when you're a young thing like you are, to be true to yourself. I know there's pressure to be on the phone, to be talking talking talking on the bus, hanging around in a gaggle like noisy geese, invited to parties every night . . .'

'Actually, I don't get invited to parties,' I said bitterly.

'Well, good!' Sheila pointed her pencil at me triumphantly. 'Good for you. You're well on your way. By the time you're twenty, you'll be partying like I do. Just you and a pork pie. Because people like you and me have worked out your own company is best.'

With this final proclamation, Sheila turned her attention back to her puzzle. She carefully wrote the word CACTUS as the solution to 9 down.

When my shift was over, I took my phone out of my bag and rang Til before I was even at the end of the road.

'Til,' I said as soon as she answered. 'I need more friends. Immediately. Please do not ever let it happen that my only friend is a pork pie.'

It had occurred to me with increasing panic that even my three-year-old brother Paddy, whose best friend was a stuffed Lizard called Dustbin, had a livelier social life than me, being invited as he was to parties most weekends.

Til yawned. 'You what? Are you still sulking about the America party? It was only OK, you know. Average. It wasn't the best night ever or anything.'

'Well, that's great, isn't it! I can't even get invited to the average nights!'

'You don't like Jon-Jon,' Til said. 'And actually, didn't you say that an American diner was the last place you'd want to hang out and that you'd seen enough milkshakes and grilled meat to last a lifetime when you worked at the Ranch?'

'But, Til, that's not the point! Not liking things is my choice. Being left out of things is not!'

Til paused. 'So just to confirm my understanding is correct: you feel left out of things you don't want to do, by people you don't even like?'

'Exactly.'

Til sighed. 'Right. So, what are you going to do about it?'

'I'm going to change things! I'm going to get popular!'

PART 2:

Where I meet a bear, make a snake and become a cat

The Booth

On Monday in college, as I knew they would be, everyone was talking about the American Dream milkshake party and all I wanted to do was to go and sit on my own and glare at things and wait until it was over. However, I was aware that sitting on my own and glaring was no way to get people to like me, and I'd meant what I said to Til: I wanted to make friends. Even more than that, I wanted people to make friends with me.

The evening before, on the walk home from my shift at Podrick's, I'd begun to try to work out exactly how a person goes from being not particularly popular to popular. What I was interested in, was what exactly the *difference* was between people like me, who found themselves sitting in their bedrooms on a Saturday night watching parties on their phones, and people who always had a crowd around them. People who were invited to everything, even things they didn't want to go to. People like the ones who sat in the Booth.

The Booth was an enclosed area at the end of the canteen

with a big round table in the middle and chairs with red foam seats dotted around it. No matter what time you went into the canteen, the Booth was never empty. There was always at least one member of the Booth crowd sitting in it, and the general understanding was that other people – ordinary civilians like me and Reeta and Til – weren't welcome there. I should say that the Booth crowd weren't actively unfriendly. I had never seen them turn anyone away or be unpleasant. It was just that there was an unspoken and mysterious agreement that they were cooler than the rest of us.

Things went on amongst them that us normal people couldn't imagine. Luke Neal, for example, always wore tiny little short-sleeve shirts like he was about to star in a production of *Grease* and was so good at the drums that actual real famous singers sometimes used him in their backing band.

Lucy Harmer had a French mum and sometimes would just go over to France and go to college over there for a few weeks before coming back here and picking up where she left off, as if living in two entirely separate countries at the same time was something any of us might do.

My own personal favourite member of the Booth, given that all my knowledge came from observing them from afar, was Kendall Cross. Kendall was in my year but had taken a year out after school before coming to college to work on some kind of small business she had set up, so was a year older than everyone else. And she looked about ten years older. She had masses of blonde hair, teeth so white they could probably light the way in a caving expedition and

20

she always wore slouchy trousers that meant she walked about the place with her hands in her pockets like she was as relaxed in public as she was in her own bedroom.

I knew there was no way someone sophisticated and grownup like Kendall Cross would ever see someone like me – awkward, clumsy Grace Dart – as an equal, but I had fantasies about her one day laughing at a joke I'd made in the same way you might have a fantasy about the lead singer of your favourite band calling you up to the stage to help sing when she'd lost her voice.

I realised that Kendall, Lucy, Luke – all of the types of people who made their college base in the Booth – could be a good place for me to start my work to become popular. Not so I could approach them or anything – I wasn't about to try to climb Everest before I had even selected my walking boots, for heaven's sake – but so I could observe. Before I launched into action, I needed to make a careful study of exactly what the popular people did. I wanted to watch how they spoke, what they talked about, their mannerisms, their body language, their clothes. I decided that, as a start at least, I could do worse than position myself near the Booth and concentrate very carefully on what went on there.

I arrived at college twenty minutes before first period and set myself up at a table as near to the Booth as possible without risking anyone thinking I was trying to actually join them. I put my psychology textbook on the table to disguise my true activities, took my notebook from my bag and began to watch.

I tried hard to keep my observations detached, behaving

as I imagined David Attenborough might, as he watched hippos gathering around a watering hole.

8.15 a.m.
Molly Shaw and Luke Neal sit side-by-side at one end of the Booth. M Shaw eats a yoghurt – variety not visible from current vantage point. L Neal lies on table, head resting on arm. Body language clear – 'I am relaxed, this is my area'. M Shaw wears hairpiece with striking 'bunny ears' design – unclear if serious fashion choice or light-hearted sartorial joke.

8.30 a.m.
Lucy Harmer and an unknown female join the Booth. Again, bold style choices are on show: loose suit with bold leaf print (surely pyjamas? Investigate further), dungarees with full stripe. New arrivals kiss M Shaw in greeting – although note no direct contact appears to take place.

I had to go to my psychology class in first period but in second period I was free, so able to recommence my study. There were more of them now and it was noisier in the canteen, so it was harder to make out exactly what was going on, but I did my best to record anything that might be useful.

10.10 a.m.
Seven individuals now occupy the Booth. Body

language is relaxed but voices are loud. Clearly unconcerned about disturbance to those around them*. Clothes are bold in colour and print. Laughter is frequent and raucous.

10.15 a.m.
*Update, revision of previous theory: perhaps not just unconcerned by disturbance they cause, but are actively aiming for this? I.e., to draw attention?

'What are you up to?' Til's voice made me jump. I'd been so engrossed I hadn't seen her approach. I realised it must be break time. I covered up my notes with my arm but it was too late, she'd already noticed.

'I'm just carrying out a small study,' I told her, sitting up straight and placing my hand on my page of notes. 'I'm observing.'

'What are you observing?' she said, sitting down. 'And why?'

'I'm observing human social behaviour. Once I have gathered sufficient data I will analyse my findings and use the results to determine how best to proceed.'

'Gracie, what are you *talking* about?'

'I can't just bulldoze my way in to making new friends. I need to think and watch and come up with a careful plan.'

Til's face cleared. 'Ah, I *see*. This is your big plan to get people to like you. Starting today, is it? Why's looking at that lot going to help?' She nodded towards the Booth, where Luke Neal had climbed onto a table and started beating his chest like a gorilla.

'One moment, please.' I paused our conversation while I added a note to my page.

Surprising and rebellious gestures are common – more evidence of attention seeking?

'Because, obviously,' I said, looking up at Til again, 'they're popular. It can't be random – who's popular and who isn't – there must be some rules to it. A pattern. I just need to find out what the pattern is. So I can copy it.'

Til opened a can of Coke and took a swig. 'Or you could, I dunno, just be yourself?'

I gave Til a hard look. 'Til, we both know that is no way for someone like me to make friends.'

She didn't argue with this, I noticed.

'So, what patterns have you noticed? What's the key to it?'

'Well,' I said, flicking through my notes. 'It's been a very interesting morning. And so far, my recurring observation is that they stand out. It seems to be about attention. And something I can say for certain is that visually, each of them has a strong individual look. That seems essential. A bare minimum.'

Til looked over and raised an eyebrow. 'Yeah, they do all look like they got dressed in the dark.'

'Exactly,' I said. 'It's bold. It's original. It's unique. And it stands to reason that to set yourself up as a key player, as a *somebody*, you need to find a way to stand out from the nobodies.'

'So, that's your plan, is it? Give yourself a makeover and the invites will start flooding in?'

I sighed. This was a particular habit of Til's – trying to make fun of my ideas by deliberately misunderstanding them.

'No. Obviously not. But I think freshening up my image can't hurt, can it? I'm so boring to look at people probably mistake me for the wall. They look right through me. Close your eyes.'

'What? No. That's what Reeta always says when she wants to nick my crisps.'

'Go on, close your eyes,' I insisted and eventually Til did as she was told. 'Now tell me what I'm wearing.'

Til screwed up her face, thinking. 'Like . . . a jumper. Red? Grey?'

'Nope!' I said triumphantly and Til opened her eyes again. 'See? You can't even say what I'm wearing when you were looking at me literally ten seconds ago. I'm forgettable. Unnoticeable. And how is anyone going to want to make friends with me if they haven't even noticed I'm here? I need to be bold and interesting, to catch people's attention and get them wanting to know more. I need to stand out.'

Jeans and Jumpers and Jumpers and Jeans

That evening, I stood in front of my wardrobe, my eyes running over the hangers and shelves. I was beginning to think that creating a bold and interesting new look – one that no one else had already taken – might be easier said than done.

As things stood, I wore almost the same thing to college every day: jeans, trainers, a T-shirt. A jumper if it was cold. Everything I owned was some variety of this. I had jumpers of different colours and some of my jeans had a patch on the knee or particularly useful pockets, but they were still jumpers and jeans.

How was I going to shake things up when every item in my wardrobe had been seen by everyone I knew at least fifty times before? There was nothing exactly wrong with any of it, but the whole purpose of a re-style was to turn heads and I just wasn't sure how I was going to achieve that goal with what I had before me.

I pulled everything out of my wardrobe and my chest of drawers and spread it out on my bed. I squinted my eyes until everything became a blur of colour, trying to get some inspiration for how I could put things together in a way no one had ever seen before.

I picked up T-shirts and cardigans and jeans and jumpers and tried them on in every different combination I could think of. Some of the combinations were brighter than others and some of them looked like I was colour-blind or pattern-blind or just blind-blind, but it was still all just so . . . me. There was nothing here that was going to get people looking. To make them think there was more to me that they had realised.

I sighed. I scooped the pile of fabric into my arms and shoved everything back into the bottom of my wardrobe, not even bothering to fold or hang it.

Then I closed the wardrobe doors so I didn't have to look at the chaos and left my bedroom altogether.

If I was serious about re-launching my image, I was going to need to look further afield.

An Interesting Biscuit

The following day, as I made my walk across the college car park and into the main front doors, it occurred to me that today would be very useful, from a research point of view.

In fact, it was unfortunate that, being so personally central to this particular experiment, I wouldn't be able to watch it from the outside and make detailed notes on what was happening. Never mind, I decided. I could still make my general observations and mentally log what was happening and analyse it in detail later. And from my general observations so far, it was quite clear what was happening:

People were noticing me.

It was an unusual feeling and I'd be lying if I said it didn't make me feel a bit shy, but I knew that, on the whole, this was very good news. It was an important development.

Of course, I knew that noticing me and *liking* me weren't the same thing, but the noticing was an important first step. It was very much like what we talked about in business studies when we'd analysed manufacturer's choices of packaging: The point of putting biscuits, for example, in exciting bright packaging was to get people to notice them on the shelf. People wouldn't necessarily *buy* the biscuits because of the packaging alone, but they might stop to take a closer look. And if they liked what they saw, then *boom!* Sale made. So looking like an interesting biscuit was an important first step.

And, right now, I knew I looked like a very interesting biscuit indeed.

As I walked across the main college reception towards my locker, I saw Mac, the college caretaker, emerge from the staff toilets carrying a mop and a toolbox.

'Morning, Gracie!' he called, waving his mop and smiling. He fell into step with me. 'And how are you this morning?'

Everyone liked Mac. No one was sure how old he was because he was as wrinkly as a raisin but he bounded around the place like a Labrador, never seeming to get stiff or tired. No one was sure why he was called Mac either, or whether that was his first name or his surname or if it was just because in the winter he wore a bright yellow mac like a fisherman. He lived with his wife – Mrs Mac – in a little cottage on the field next to college.

He was the most cheerful man I had ever met. I knew some people were good at counting their cup as half full but Mac managed to look at a completely empty cup and somehow see that it was completely full of champagne that had been poured just for him.

Once, for example, I was standing near to him while he was up a ladder fixing a blind in a classroom when his phone fell out of his pocket and bounced off the corner of a table, smashing the screen into bits.

He climbed down from the ladder and picked it up from the floor, but rather than swearing or moaning about how much it was going to cost to fix like most people would have, he just smiled and said, 'Well, isn't that lucky? Just this morning the old boy in the paper shop told me he was starting to do phone screen repairs. '

'I'm fine,' I said, in answer to his question now. 'Just ordinary, you know.'

'Well, you don't look ordinary!' From anyone else this might have felt like an insult but not from Mac with his wide grin showing his missing bottom tooth. 'You look extraordinary!'

'Do I?' I said.

'Yes!' he said. 'You know what it is – it's avant-garde. I just learnt that expression the other day. Came across it in one of my articles and looked it up. I'm sure a brain-box like you already knows what it means though.'

I frowned. I'd heard it before, I was sure, but I couldn't quite recall the exact definition. I shook my head. 'Don't think I do.'

'It means forward!' Mac said, thrusting his mop forward like he was in a jousting match. 'It means ahead of the game! Trailblazing! Setting the world alight with your new ideas!'

'Does it?'

'Yep,' he nodded. 'That's what you're doing today. I can see. And good for you, girl!' And with that, he turned sharply to the left and went into a classroom to do whatever jobs he needed to do, waving his mop and calling, 'Have a good day, trailblazer!'

I was glad I'd met Mac so early in the day and received such a positive response to my new image. It meant that rather than feeling nervous as I made my way to my locker, I felt energised. I was avant-garde! A trailblazer!

Reeta was already by the lockers when I arrived. Her eyes widened as soon as she saw me.

'Gracie, what happened?' she said, putting her hand on my arm.

'What?' I said. 'How do you mean?'

'I mean, to your house?' she said, her eyes running over me from head to foot. 'Did it burn down? Or did they find an unexploded bomb nearby and the police knocked on your door and said, "Everybody, evacuate this street at once!" and you all had to just grab whatever you could carry and run for your lives?'

'What on earth are you talking about, please?'

'Gracie, where are your clothes!' she wailed, throwing her hands up in the air.

I frowned at her. 'Well, here. On my body. Quite clearly. I'm not standing here nude, am I?'

Reeta reached out and touched my sleeve, holding the fabric between her thumb and finger. 'But these aren't . . . yours?'

I tossed my hair in a gesture designed to demonstrate how casual and relaxed I was about my new image.

'It's not a big deal. You're just surprised because you're used to seeing me in the same thing every day. But there's really nothing strange about wearing a new outfit once in a while.'

I badly wanted to feel as comfortable as I was pretending I

was. I tried to tell myself that Reeta was only so shocked and perplexed by my outfit because she was always shocked and perplexed. (Once, for example, she had run into class with panic in her eyes because she thought a boy's head had twisted all the way around when all that had happened was that he'd put his coat on back to front.) But my confidence was slipping away with every moment she stared at me, her mouth slightly open. Perhaps I should have stuck to my own wardrobe after all.

Just then, Til arrived at the lockers. She stopped walking abruptly as soon as she saw me, her eyebrows raised so high that they started to get mixed in with her hair.

'Gracie. WHAT is going on here. What have you done to your hair?'

'I just dyed it.'

'What with? Blood?'

'No. Red food colouring. We didn't have any dye and it's much the same, I'm sure.'

Til just blinked. 'And the . . . clothes?'

I sighed and turned away to open my locker. 'Oh, for goodness' sake! It's just a T-shirt dress!'

Til continued to look at me. 'Well, it's a T-shirt, anyway. And what is that pattern? Is it . . . are they haddocks?'

'They're tropical fish! It's a tropical fish T-shirt dress!'

'Gracie, a T-shirt doesn't become a T-shirt dress just because you don't bother to put trousers on.'

I paused. 'Yes, it does. Doesn't it?'

Til shook her head. Then her expression shifted slightly. Sympathy. 'Is it your dad's?' she asked gently.

'Technically. He never wears it though.' Even as I said it I knew this was perhaps beside the point.

'Is the hat his as well?' Reeta asked, nodding to my plastic sun visor with the neon green peak.

'No, of course not!' I snapped. 'My dad isn't going to wear a neon visor, is he?' Then I added, more quietly. 'It's Paddy's.'

'And the socks? They're Paddy's too, are they?' Til said and Reeta crouched right down to get a look at my Peppa Pig socks, which I had planned to stretch up to my knees but as they were only little, had to make do with just past my ankle. I had to admit, it was a tricky length to pull off.

'He was very happy to lend them to me,' I said quietly.

'So, and just as a matter of pure curiosity,' Til said, the corner of her mouth twitching, 'why *have* you chosen to come to college wearing your dad's worst T-shirt, your baby brother's hat and socks, and – most interestingly of all – no trousers?'

I threw my arms up in the air. 'Why? Because why not! Why are you wearing that . . . that jumper! Why are you wearing those boots! I wear what I want when I want because I am Gracie Dart, I'm one of a kind and I will not follow the crowd!'

Til didn't reply to my outburst. She just nodded slowly and continued looking at me, her nose twitching like a nervous rabbit, in that way it does when she's trying hard not to laugh.

'Is this about Gracie trying to be popular still?' Reeta whispered to her.

'I have no idea,' Til whispered back.

33

A Surprise

Til had two free periods after lunch so she went home for the afternoon, but just as I was leaving college she sent me a message:

Til: All right Winnie the Pooh. Come round mine later, I've got something to show you.

Me: Why are you calling me Winnie the Pooh?

Til: Because he doesn't wear trousers

Me: Neither does Donald Duck

Til: Fine. Just come over later, Donald.

Me: Why?

Til: Don't want to ruin the surprise. And it is *quite* surprising.

Even though I knew Til was taking advantage of my natural curiosity to boss me about, I wanted to see what she was talking about, so that evening I walked up the hill to her flat.

Til lived on the ninth floor of a block of flats just back from the pier. It was just her and her mum there, and although there were times I would have quite liked to be an only child with no annoying brothers getting in my way and leaving their stuff everywhere, I knew there were parts of her life she would have liked to swap with mine. Her mum, for example, had quite massive mood swings, sometimes crying in bed for days and sometimes getting the sack from her job for shouting at people. I wasn't sure if she'd be home tonight.

As Til opened the door, she held her fingers to her lips. 'Shh.'

'Why?' I said, but keeping my voice down as requested. 'Is your mum in bed?'

Til shook her head. 'She's not here.'

'So why . . . ?'

'Tell you in a minute,' she whispered. 'Do you want a drink?'

I followed Til into the kitchen, where she closed the door behind us.

'Got your trousers on now then?' she said, her voice a little above a whisper now, but still quiet.

'I've got changed, yes,' I said coolly. 'With hindsight I realised that was more of a summer look.'

'And did it work? Are you popular now? Are people following you around the corridors like you're the Pied Piper?'

'You're so annoying,' I said, my efforts to keep my voice

35

down making it come out a bit like a hiss. 'Why can't you ever be a supportive friend? It's all right for you with your plumbing mates, and getting invited to all the parties even though you make zero effort ever. I've got to try. I'm more of an acquired taste.'

'Like olives?'

'Exactly like olives, actually. And as I've already explained, all I wanted was for a few people to notice me for once.'

Til held up her hands, her palms facing me. 'OK, OK, I'm sorry. You have my full support. But did it work? Did people notice you?'

'I don't know. Well, I mean, yes, they looked. And I think some of them sort of . . . sniggered . . . but I don't know that it's going to really work the way I hoped. I mean, I know it's early days and I should go home and find something else interesting to wear tomorrow because you can't really call something a new image if you've only worn it for one day but I don't know if it's going to make any difference. People are *looking* at me, but no one's actually spoken to me. No one new anyway. Do you think maybe it's too late?' I took the glass of squash she was holding out for me. 'Do you think people already formed their impressions of me the day they met me and now it's too late to undo them?'

'No idea,' Til said, downing her drink in one.

'Oh,' I said.

'I think,' Til said, refilling her glass, 'that you're underestimating the task you've set yourself. To be honest, I thought that right when you said it, when you called me to tell me you're going to be popular now. Because, you

36

know, you can't just *decide* to be popular, go home and put on your "look at me I'm popular" T-shirt, then that's that. People spend their whole *lives* trying to be popular and still never make it. It's a lifelong mission.'

I sighed. Maybe she was right. 'Anyway. What did you want to show me? And why are we having to be so quiet?'

She didn't say anything, but she opened the kitchen door once again, putting her finger to her lips. She crossed the hall to the bathroom and beckoned me over. I gave her a questioning look but she just gently opened the bathroom door and stood there, looking in.

I went to stand behind her and look over her shoulder.

'A bear!' I hadn't meant to shout so loudly but the surprise got the better of me.

The sound of my voice startled the bear, and the big ball of fluff that had been curled up in the bath scrambled to its feet and launched itself at me, big paws pushing into my stomach, enormous pink tongue flapping about trying to get at my face.

'This is why I wanted to be quiet!' Til said, wrestling the animal away from me. 'She's easier when she's asleep. Get down, girl. Down!'

'Why have you got a bear!' I said, as Til managed to persuade the animal to stop trying to climb up me and it stood in the middle of the bathroom, its tail thumping against the towel rail.

'Well, it's not a bear, it's a dog. Obviously,' Til said.

'Is it obvious?' I said. 'It looks more like a bear to me. And still, why? Why is it here? And why is it so . . . big? Is it a normal dog? It's *part* bear, surely?'

'It's a Newfoundland. They're massive. Maybe crossed with something. She's a rescue so we can't really be sure.'

'And she's . . . yours, now, is she?' I was quite taken aback. Surely people don't just go home from college one day and pick up a bear or a dog or whatever it was.

Til nodded. 'Yep. Looks like it. One of Mum's friends got her, but she couldn't cope and so Mum said we'd have her. She didn't bother checking with me first, of course. Even though Mum's at work six days a week so I'm the one stuck indoors with her.'

'Oh.' I blinked. I didn't know what to make of it all. 'OK.'

'She is cute, in a way,' Til said. 'But she's just so massive and she's got so much energy. And this flat is tiny.'

'Yeah . . .' Already I could see dog hair all over the furniture and our clothes. 'What's her name?'

'Lady.'

'Lady?'

'Gaga.'

'Lady Gaga?'

Til nodded. 'Yep. Mum's mate is a big fan.'

This made me laugh loudly and Lady Gaga looked at me for a moment with her head on one side. Then she bounced over to me and I rubbed her huge head.

'So are you OK about it? If you have to walk her and stuff?'

Til shrugged. 'I guess I have to be. And yeah, I think I am. Because Mum is so happy with her. And honestly, anything that makes my mum happy can only make my life easier.'

Making Things Happen

At college the next day, Reeta and I sat in the computer lab helping Til search for video tutorials that would explain how she could train Lady Gaga not to put her front paws on the side in the kitchen and steal food from plates.

I was back in my normal clothes, so I was more comfortable, but I felt despondent. Til was right, I knew, that I couldn't just decide to be popular and the next day be surrounded by people and invitations. I was willing to put in the work, but I wasn't sure exactly what that work should be.

Perhaps there was nothing I could do. It was just fate, whether people liked you or not. Stupid random luck. And I found that hard to accept. I was a person who liked to take control. To make things happen.

I turned to Reeta, who was watching a video of a Great Dane eating an apple crumble with its paws.

'You're popular,' I said. It came out sounding more like an accusation than I'd meant it to. 'People are always coming to talk to you and inviting you to things. Til says it's a lifelong mission, to be popular. Have you made it your lifelong mission?'

Reeta thought about this for a moment. Then she shook her head. 'I don't think so.'

'So what it is?' I demanded. 'What's your secret?'

She shrugged. 'Most of the people I know are from running club. Or from some other club, or because I've played a volleyball match with them or something like that. I didn't go looking for friends. I just went looking for people to play sports with.'

I nodded, weighing up this idea. 'That makes sense. You did an activity together first, then became friends later.'

'Exactly,' Reeta said.

'Interesting,' I said, tapping my finger on the table as I thought about this. 'So really, I've been thinking about things the wrong way around. I was looking to make friends *then* get invited to the activities. When really what I need to do is just turn up, do the activities, and then let everyone decide to like me afterwards.'

'Or not,' Til said.

I ignored her. 'So, what activity can I do?' I looked around the room as if there might be a table-tennis tournament or roller disco starting up as we spoke.

Til winced as the dog on the video she was watching took the corner of a tablecloth in its mouth and pulled a whole roast dinner onto the floor. 'We could go to the chip shop on the way home,' she suggested without looking up. 'That's an activity. In fact, if you count walking there, ordering the chips and eating the chips, that's three activities.'

I sighed. 'Yeah, but it can't be just *us*, Til. That's not the point. I need to do activities with other people. I thought you understood this. You two have other people. I don't.'

Til made a 'hmph' noise but she didn't offer any other ideas.

'In art, Katie was talking about a *Jaws* night she's having tonight,' Reeta said.

'Katie Boyd?' I said.

I'd known Katie for years. She was quiet and I'd never given any serious thought to being friends with her, but then that was my whole problem really, wasn't it – not enough serious effort. And at this stage, it wasn't about finding people I definitely wanted to be friends with. It was about joining in with activities – any activities that were going – and letting the friendships follow naturally after that. And if this was an event – a 'night' – there'd be lots of people there and that was lots of people who might decide I was OK after all and ask me to be friends.

'Where did she go after art?' I asked.

Reeta shrugged. 'The library, I think. But I only overheard her talking about the *Jaws* thing. She said her parents are away for two days with her sister, so she's got the whole house to herself. I'm not invited or anything. So I can't get you invited.'

'Never mind about that,' I said, getting to my feet. 'Invitations are a luxury I can't afford at this stage.'

An Invitation

I intercepted Katie just as she was leaving the library and heading down the stairs.

'Hey! Katie!' I shouted as I came up to meet her.

She looked up, surprised. 'Oh. Hi, Grace. You . . . OK?' she said. Her tone told me this roughly translated as: do you want something?

I couldn't blame her. Katie and I had been to the same school since we were tiny, but we'd never really talked to each other. We were just two people who knew each other's names. I knew that approaching her like this was unusual so I decided to just get to the point.

'So, sorry to bother you and everything, it's just that I heard that you're having some people over later, to watch *Jaws*? Like a *Jaws* night?'

She opened her mouth slightly, as if surprised.

'Oh. Well, yeah. I mean –'

It wasn't a comfortable situation. I wasn't comfortable and I could see Katie wasn't comfortable. But I knew nothing would change if I didn't force myself out of my

42

comfort zone sometimes. I was just going to have to push on through.

'So I was wondering,' I continued brightly, 'would it be OK if I kind of . . . tagged along and came over too? I mean, that would be OK, wouldn't it? One extra person? It's just, I really love *Jaws*. It's probably in my all-time top-ten favourite films if I really think about it. Well, top twenty-five at least. I just love all the sharks and all the running away from the sharks and all the . . . jaws. The jaws on those sharks are amazing, aren't they! And obviously I've seen it lots of times before – I mean, of course I have, it's in my top twenty-five best ever films – but it's just so much better to watch it with other people so you can all scream at the same time and all that. So, what I'm saying is, if you're having a *Jaws* night then I'd really love to come.'

She blinked and there was a brief pause but then she said, 'OK.' She nodded slowly. 'Why not. Sure.'

I beamed to show her she wouldn't regret her generosity. 'Great! Do you still live on Seven Dials? What time shall we say?'

With the details confirmed, I went to find Til and Reeta to share the news of my success.

'See,' I said, after I told them what had happened. 'My first invitation. Told you I could get them if I wanted them.'

Til made a face. 'Well, your first invitation if you count invitations from yourself.'

I waved my hand. 'She said I could go. She said I could go to her house and watch a film with her. That's an invitation. All I did was plant the seed of the idea. Then she was more than happy to have me along.'

Jaws Night

At seven-fifteen I arrived at Katie's house holding a carrier bag containing one bottle of lemonade, a bag of Doritos, a bag of popcorn, three tubs of Pringles and a chocolate dinosaur that had been on offer at the till. I didn't know how many people Katie was expecting for the evening, but I decided that showing people how generous I was could only be a good thing.

Katie opened the door and straight away I realised she looked rather glamorous. Her hair was all swooshy, like she'd spent time both straightening it out and puffing it up, and she was wearing a sparkly little top and bangles around her wrists. I looked down at my own sweatshirt – a loose thread on the sleeve and a small splash of ketchup on the front. I hadn't realised it was a dressing-up kind of party. I wondered for a minute if I should go home and change but I decided there was no need. It would probably be dark once she put the film on, and everyone would be looking at the screen then anyway.

'Is anyone else here yet?' I asked as Katie let me in the front door and led me down the corridor to her lounge. I put my bag of snacks in the corner.

She shook her head. 'No,' she said. 'Just you.' Then she added, 'I wasn't sure you'd come, really. I thought you might forget.'

I couldn't see how anyone could forget a social engagement when there were less than five hours between arranging it and it beginning, but I decided maybe she didn't have people over a lot. In fact, she seemed so tense about the whole thing that I decided the kindest thing to do was to babble away for a bit to put her mind at ease.

'Oh, I know,' I said. 'I always get nervous when I invite people to things. Even when they say they're going to come, people often drop out at the last minute and don't show, don't they? It's so inconsiderate. Although,' I added after a pause, 'normally I've only invited Til and sometimes I'm hoping she doesn't show, to be honest.'

Katie nodded but I got the feeling she wasn't completely listening to me. She stood in the middle of the room, looking around carefully like she was surveying it. She stepped forward and moved a cushion from one chair to another, then after stepping back to assess her change, she moved it back again.

'Well, I've not really invited that many people,' she said, wiping some dust off the mantlepiece with a tissue from a box on the coffee table.

'Probably for the best,' I said. I sat down and took a bag of Doritos out of my carrier bag. 'Always easier to manage a select gathering. Don't want people chatting all over the film.'

She frowned slightly but didn't say anything. I offered her the bag of Doritos but she shook her head and went to stand by the window. She hugged her arms around her chest as she looked out. I wished she'd just relax a bit. Why have people over if you find it so stressful?

When the doorbell eventually rang, she jumped like a startled pony.

'Want me to get it?' I said, shifting myself forward on the sofa in a move to get to my feet.

'No!' she said quickly, shaking her head and holding out her arm as if to physically prevent me from getting up. 'No. It's OK.'

'Fair enough.' I leant back on the sofa and carried on with my Doritos.

I heard her open the door. 'Hey!' a voice said. 'Sorry I'm late.'

I recognised that voice easily: Martin.

I stood up and went to greet him in the doorway to the lounge. 'Hi, Martin!' I called down the corridor. I pushed another handful of crisps into my mouth. It really was hard to stop eating those things once you got going. 'I didn't know you were coming!'

Martin looked at me for a moment and opened his mouth as if to say something. Then he closed it again, and looked at Katie. When she just shrugged, he finally spoke. 'Grace! Hi!'

I suppose it was no surprise that he hadn't been expecting

to see me – I wasn't in Katie's usual crowd after all – but from his reaction you'd think I'd been resurrected from the dead. I realised then that things were worse than I thought if I was considered so much of a recluse that people were visibly shocked to see me at something as ordinary as a film evening.

Martin came into the hall and passed a carrier bag to Katie. She peered inside and smiled, then took it away to the kitchen. More snacks, I guessed. We weren't going to need to eat again for a week at this rate.

Martin came to join me in the lounge and took a seat in the corner of one sofa.

'So, Grace . . .' he said, rubbing the knees of his jeans with his palms. He too seemed quite dressed up, I noticed. I could see the creases on his T-shirt sleeves where he'd obviously ironed it. 'You here to watch the film then?'

I nodded. 'Uh-huh.'

Martin nodded back, but he didn't say anything else. He was acting oddly, I thought. It wasn't like him to seem so . . . nervous.

Katie came back into the room and handed Martin and me a drink each. 'So,' she said. 'I guess we might as well . . . get started?' She picked up a remote and pressed a few buttons and the TV in the corner flashed into life.

I frowned. 'Aren't we going to wait for the others?'

Katie shook her head. She wasn't looking at me. She was concentrating hard on the screen. 'This is it. This is us.'

'Oh,' I said quietly. I felt bad then, for bringing so many snacks and highlighting the smallness of the gathering. And

47

I felt embarrassed too, for Katie. It was so awkward when you'd made an event out to be a big deal and then hardly anyone turned up in the end.

I sat on the floor, my back resting against the sofa, and Katie and Martin sat behind me. Katie started the film and within a couple of minutes a woman was running towards the sea, ripping off her clothes, and I sighed and shook my head, knowing it wasn't going to end well.

Despite my claim that *Jaws* was one of my all-time favourites, I'd never actually seen it before, but I was pleased to discover that it was actually very engrossing. When it got to the part where everyone thinks the shark has been caught and so goes into the water but you know that really it's still out there somewhere, I turned around to look at Katie and Martin. I think I'd been planning on doing a kind of face at them – a kind of 'eek something's going to go wrong here!' face – because I was feeling the evening was a bit lacking in camaraderie. I'd thought the whole point of watching these scary movies together was that you all went 'ooh' and 'ahh' and 'noooo' at the same time, which was a bit more fun than just sitting and watching them in silence in your own bedroom. But when I turned to look at them, after my eyes had adjusted to the dim light, I realised that Katie's head was on Martin's chest, and his arm was draped over her shoulder.

'Oh!' I said before I could stop myself. When they realised that I was looking at them, Martin quickly removed his arm and Katie sat up, which only made the whole situation even clearer.

'Oh!' I said again. 'Oh, I see. I –'

I stopped. Katie and Martin looked at each other. They didn't say anything.

'So you're . . . are you two . . . boyfriends? I mean, girlfriends! I mean, boyfriend and girlfriend!' I said. 'Dating?'

Martin looked at Katie. She chewed on her lip. From the TV came a voice delivered over a loud speaker. 'Everybody, please get out of the water.'

'Well, we haven't really . . .' Katie began.

'I'm not sure that . . .' Martin said.

'It's not official but . . .' Katie looked at Martin and they both laughed suddenly.

Then Martin said, 'I mean, we sort of *are* dating. In that this is the first date . . .'

'Oh my god,' I said, scrambling to my feet.

'Well,' he went on. 'I mean, I thought that's what it was, but then I wasn't expecting you to be here, Grace, to be completely honest, so maybe I got the wrong idea . . .' He looked at Katie. 'It was just when you said . . . did I want to come over . . . I sort of assumed . . . But maybe I got it wrong.'

Katie shook her head. 'No,' she said quickly. 'You didn't. I did mean that, when I asked you. It's just . . .'

'Oh god,' I said again. 'I invited myself. I've invited myself to your first date. I'm so sorry. I'm *so* sorry.' I looked around the room for my coat, eventually grabbing it from the arm of a chair. 'I'm gone,' I said. 'Pretend I wasn't ever here.' I went to retrieve my carrier bag of snacks but then I decided that leaving it with them was the least I could do. 'Tell me what happens in the film,' I said, as

49

I crossed the room to the door. But then, remembering I was supposedly already a fan, added, 'I mean, *I* know what happens, obviously, but tell me what you think of it . . . if you like it and . . . OK, I'm going. Have a nice time. Goodbye! Bye!'

Before they could say anything, I left the lounge, closing the door behind me.

As I passed the kitchen, I saw what Martin had handed Katie when he'd arrived: a single red rose.

The Date Crasher

'It's not that funny,' I said when Til had been laughing for so long and so loudly that some foreign students at the back of the bus had stopped their conversation to look over at us. Reeta, Til and I were on our way to college, the day after my date-crashing, gate-crashing disaster.

'It is! It's just so typical of you, to try so hard to make yourself popular you end up doing the one thing that could make you even more *un*popular. Wonder if Katie or Martin will ever speak to you again!'

'Shut up,' I said. Although I knew she had a point. 'But anyway, I'm putting it behind me. And I've been thinking: maybe it's time I thought seriously about sport.'

'Sport!' Reeta sat up excitedly like a puppy that'd spotted a squirrel.

Til pulled a face. 'You what?'

'Purely as a means to an end,' I mean.

When Reeta had listed her sporting activities as her main source of friendship, I hadn't even considered it could be an option for me. Not liking sports, and more specifically being *bad* at sports, had been part of my character for so long I couldn't imagine changing it any more than I could imagine growing an extra pair of ears. But then, it had been a long time since I'd actually *tried* any sport.

There was PE at school, but there had always been ways to get around that – a forgotten pair of trainers here, a feigned ankle injury there – so I don't think I'd so much as broken a sweat since Year Seven. Maybe, if I actually tried, and found a sport that was fun and that wasn't led by an angry lady with whiskers on her chin and a tracksuit she'd bought in 1986, I might not be so bad. And it did seem like sports were a good way to make friends. It certainly explained why Reeta was so in demand.

'Because who's to say that I am actually bad at sports?' I said, turning round in my seat to look at Reeta and Til.

'You,' Reeta said. 'You always say it.'

'And Mrs Bosworth and Mr Lee and every PE teacher we've ever had,' Til said.

'A-ha! But that's just the thing!' I said, jabbing my finger in the air like a scientist making a discovery. 'They never actually said "Grace Dart, you are bad at sports" did they? They said "Grace Dart, you are not making any effort" or "Grace Dart you're serving a tennis ball, not flipping a pancake". They were talking about my attitude, not my *aptitude*. And anyway, that was all ages ago. Years ago, some of it. And I'm talking about the here and now.'

'So, in the here and now, you're good at sports, are you?' Til said. 'Got any evidence for this claim?'

'I didn't say I was definitely good. Just that I'm not necessarily bad. We just don't know either way at the moment. But the important point is, I'm ready to try again. Because I think Reeta's right; it does seem a good way to meet people. And also I do want to get fit! I'm not getting any younger, you know.'

'Which sport will you do, Gracie?' Reeta asked.

'Well, that's what I wanted to ask you. You've sampled a lot. What do you recommend? For me, I mean?'

Reeta squinted and looked out of the window. 'A good sport for a beginner . . .'

'Well, not a complete beginner,' I pointed out. 'Think of me as someone coming out of retirement.'

'How about yoga?' Reeta said, turning back to look at me. 'It's very good for all bodies and all levels. You can't really ever get it wrong.'

I scrunched up my nose. 'Yoga? Isn't it all humming and breathing and sighing? I'm not sure it's really a sport at all, if you really think about it.'

'Oh, it is,' Reeta said, nodding earnestly. 'It's quite tiring actually, with some of the shapes you have to bend into. You have to be quite strong to get really good at it. There's a class in St Barnabas Church that I usually go to on a Wednesday. You can come with me, if you like?'

I thought about this. I wasn't wild about the idea of all that bending and stretching but then that wasn't the point. 'What are the people like there? The people who do it. They're nice, are they?'

Reeta nodded. 'Yep. All nice. No one not nice.'

That sounded promising, at least.

'OK,' I said. 'You're on. I'll give it a go.'

A Whimpering Noise

When I got home from college that evening, the house was strangely quiet.

Normally my older brother Ollie would be shuffling about the place in his old-man slippers, Paddy would be parading up and down the hallway in a princess dress or hosting a dinner party for his soft toys, and either Mum or Dad – whoever had come home early to look after Paddy – would be trying to carry the laundry basket up the stairs, while at the same time shouting, 'But, Mrs Thunderbolt! How will I ever get out if you don't come to rescue me!' or whatever line was required of them in order to stay in character according to Paddy's game.

But that night, no one was home at all. At least, that's what I thought, until I heard a whimpering noise coming from upstairs that sounded like a small kitten had got stuck under a piece of furniture. I armed myself with an umbrella from the stand by the door in case it turned out to be an actually quite large kitten, or worse, an intruder trying to lull me into a false sense of security by doing an impression of a kitten, and I headed upstairs.

'Is someone there?' I called from halfway up.

'Grace?' came the reply, which I suppose ruled out the kitten.

The noise was coming from the bathroom. Carefully, I pushed open the door.

'Mum!'

She was lying on the floor. Luckily with a towel wrapped round all the important parts.

'Thank god you're home,' she said in a small voice.

'What are you doing down there?'

'Back's gone,' she said. Her voice was muffled by the way her head was turned, her mouth pushed against the floor. 'I could feel it was stiff so I came home from work early and decided to have a bath to see if I could relax the muscles. But then I slipped getting out and . . . well, now it's well and truly gone.'

'Can you get up?' I said, crouching down next to her.

Mum shuffled a little bit but cried out in pain before she got anywhere. 'No. I think I'll need Dad and Ollie to lift me. But I'm more worried about Paddy.'

'Where is he?'

'He's at Maureen's still. I keep hearing my phone go so she's obviously wondering where I am but I can't get to it. Can you go and pick him up?'

Maureen was the woman who lived four doors down who picked Paddy up from nursery and looked after him until Mum or Dad finished work.

'Yeah, of course. But what about you? I can't just leave you here?'

'Just get me the duvet from the spare bed – I'm freezing down here – then I'll be OK till the boys get home. Dad should be on his way by now.'

It felt strange to be tucking Mum up under a duvet in the middle of the bathroom floor but I didn't see what else I could do. So once she assured me again that she'd be all right for a while longer, I headed out to collect Paddy from Maureen's.

When we got home, I was relieved to find that Dad and Ollie had both returned and the operation to retrieve Mum from the bathroom floor was already underway.

I hovered in the hallway.

'Do you need me?' I asked.

'I think we're OK,' Dad said, his voice straining with the effort of trying to lift Mum without making any sudden movements. 'Just keep an eye on Paddy, would you?'

Downstairs, I kept Paddy occupied by playing one of his favourite games, Lizard Walk.

Paddy's latest preoccupation was lizards, particularly the way they scuttled across the floor, and the game involved both of us getting on all fours and imitating the walk. If Paddy decided that the walk fell below standards, your punishment was the Lizard Tongue, where he got close to your face, darted out his tongue and licked you. If you did it well enough, you were allowed to continue Lizard Walking uninterrupted.

When Mum was safely in bed, and Dad was downstairs

making her a cup of tea, I went in to see her. 'Are you OK?'

She gave me a weak smile. 'Better now I'm in bed rather than on the floor.'

'Do you think you should go to hospital?'

Mum laughed. 'No, darling. Just rest. It's just a pain in the bum because we've got so much on at the moment. Visitors, Paddy's birthday. I'll need to rearrange it all.'

'The visitors can just come to your room and sit on your bed and fan you with palm leaves and read novels to you in a calming voice. That's what they did for the feeble and sickly in history.'

'Sounds tempting,' Mum said. 'Can you get me my phone? I need to sort a few things.'

'Leave that now,' Dad said, as he came into the room with the tea. 'It'll all wait till tomorrow. You just need to rest.'

Mum groaned. 'But there's so much to do! You can't do it all on your own.'

'I'm not on my own,' Dad said. 'Oliver and Grace are here. You're more than happy to help, aren't you?' He gave me a pointed look.

'Oh,' I said. 'Yeah. Totally. I love helping.' But already I was heading back to my room to try to work out exactly what one was supposed to wear to one's first ever yoga class.

My First Yoga

As I made my way to St Barnabas Church with Reeta that evening, I had a clear picture in my mind of how things would go when we arrived.

There would, I assumed, be five or six of us, girls of about our age mostly, milling around in comfy clothes. A warm, friendly and slightly eccentric woman covered in loose, brightly coloured fabrics would sit in the middle of us all, directing us how to stretch out our arms and legs in the most relaxing way possible, offering plenty of enthusiastic support and encouragement. In between the stretching there would be lots of good-natured chat and at some point the teacher would say something like, 'We're like a little family here, Grace, as you can see!' and they would all agree they were glad I'd come along.

However, when we arrived, Reeta directed me to the front of the hall to announce my presence to Petra, the teacher, and I could see at once she wasn't what I'd expected. She was very thin and her deeply tanned skin seemed to be stretched so tightly over her skeleton it was almost as if there hadn't been enough to cover it. Her hair was tied back in a severe ponytail and she had heavy black make-up around her eyes. She looked up from her list as I approached, but she didn't smile.

'My friend Reeta said it would be OK if I joined in today?' I said tentatively.

She peered at me closely. 'Have you done it before? A yoga class?' Still she didn't smile.

'Well, not a class,' I admitted. 'Not an official one. But when I'm lying in bed at night, I often see how far I can stretch out and I can make myself really long sometimes – my feet go right over the end of the bed. So I shouldn't think I'll have any problems.'

Petra seemed unimpressed. She gave me a hard stare for a moment, then she said, 'This is Yoga Plus. It's for students at an intermediate level. Beginners' class is on Tuesdays.'

I panicked. I hadn't imagined I might be turned away before I'd even begun. I didn't want to come back on Tuesday without Reeta. I wanted to do it now.

'I mean, I do yoga all the time at home,' I said quickly. 'With a DVD and things. It's just not in an official class. I normally –'

'Show me the cat,' Petra said suddenly.

I blinked. I looked down towards my bag, wondering if she was accusing me of smuggling a pet into the room.

'The cat pose,' she said again, her eyes narrowing suspiciously.

'Oh!' I said, realising what she meant. This was a test. She was setting me an entrance exam.

59

'The cat . . .' I said, nodding slowly. I had no idea what that meant, but then I decided I had nothing to lose by having a go. Paddy was often asking me to take the role of animals in his games. What would I do if he asked me to be a cat?

I got down on all fours, then I looked up at Petra, who was now standing with her hands on her hips, eyeing me critically.

'What else?' she said. 'That's not the whole cat, is it?'

I was amused that I had managed to get it half right through guess-work alone. Who needed to come to classes when you could just pretend to be an animal in your own time?

'The whole cat . . .' I said, quietly, trying to work out what else could be required.

'Yes. What do you do next?' she said. She was getting impatient now.

'Miii-aaaooooow?' I said hopefully, drawing out the sound to make it as authentic as possible.

Petra rolled her eyes, but she seemed to be bored of me.

'If you can't keep up, you'll have to leave,' she said, then abruptly turned away and clapped her hands to get the room's attention.

'OK, everyone,' she called. 'Usual drill. No more than five to a row please.'

Petra shooed me away from the front of the room and I found a spare mat next to Reeta.

'So, let's start with the tree today,' Petra said. 'One foot, as a high as you can manage against the inside leg.' She stood on one leg, bent the other one at the knee and pushed her foot against the inside of her thigh. 'Reach up tall, feeling that pull, all the way up the spine and through –'

'Argh!' I screamed as I fell over and everyone turned to look at me. 'Sorry,' I said, looking around at them all. 'Really sorry. It's just . . . harder than it looks, isn't it? To balance on one leg . . .'

I struggled to get myself back into position.

'Don't try to put the foot too high up the leg,' Petra said disapprovingly. 'Only go as high as the ankle. If that's all you can manage.'

I tried again, concentrating harder this time, but once more, as soon as I was on one leg, I toppled to the side.

Perhaps I had an inner-ear difficulty, I thought. Maybe I had a medical reason why it just wasn't possible for me to balance properly. But then, was it normal to stand on one leg like a flamingo all day? If it was, then surely you'd see it more often – people standing on one leg as they waited in the queue at the bus stop and so on – if it really was so easy, and so good for you?

'Of course,' Petra said, looking in my direction, 'in the beginner class we have support rails, but I don't bring them on Wednesdays – as this is Yoga *Plus*.'

I felt my cheeks burn as they always do when I'm being told off, but then I reminded myself: I wasn't there to be good at yoga. I didn't really care about the actual yoga at all. I was there to meet new people and to get them to be my friends.

I looked around the room. To my right was a girl I guessed was a few years older than me, with dark brown hair in a bun and bright pink leggings. It would be good, I decided, to have an older friend. She could take me to cool parties and introduce me to music I'd never heard of and offer me wise advice about life after college. I decided to make her my target.

When we finally finished doing our impressions of a tree, Petra said it was time to become a triangle. I quickly realised this offered me an opportunity.

The triangle pose basically meant standing with your legs quite far apart and then leaning your upper body over to one side. So I waited until the girl next to me – my target – was in position, leaning helpfully towards me, and I leant the opposite way, so at the peak of the lean, our heads were quite close together.

'Hello,' I whispered, so as not to attract Petra's attention.

The girl's eyes flickered in my direction and she gave me a small smile but she didn't say anything.

What should I say next? I thought. 'What's your name' seemed a bit childish, and anyway, there was plenty of time to gather the basics later. What I needed to do first was to say something to catch her interest, to make her want to take the conversation further.

'Triangles are my favourite shape,' I said, still whispering. Again, the girl smiled, perhaps a little more tightly this time, but then, as directed by Petra, she stretched upwards and over to the other side, and she was lost to me.

My next chance came when Petra announced it was time for us to get into the 'child's pose'. I watched while everyone around me knelt on the floor then leant forward, their arms stretched out in front of them. I wasn't sure what kind of children they were spending time with but I'd never seen any of the ones I knew get into this position. Still, it was easy enough, and a relief after all the balancing. At this point I found that, once again, my head was near enough to the girl's to attempt conversation.

'Not sure I'd call this the "child",' I whispered. 'More like the praying mantis! Well, praying something anyway. I'm not sure what a mantis is, actually. It's a bit like a big hippo, isn't it? Or is that a manatee? Or –'

'Breathing!' Petra shouted suddenly, making me jerk my head upwards. 'If you're breathing properly – which you should be, as that's at least seventy per cent of the point of being here – then you will not be able to talk!'

The girl gave me an apologetic smile and I put my head back into position facing the ground.

Yoga, I was realising, was surprisingly difficult and boring. And it seemed to go on for hours! All the poses started to blur into one after a while – standing up tall, lying out long, pretending to be whatever random word came into Petra's head. 'Now be a mountain!', 'Now be a dog!', 'Now be a Cornish pasty!'.

The bit of the class that I liked best was where it was time to do the 'relaxation pose', which basically meant lying on the floor and breathing. Frankly, I thought it was a bit of a con that Petra was charging us all five pounds just so we could lie flat on our backs and breathe in and out for three minutes. Which, not meaning to boast, I was already pretty much an expert at.

Finally, the class was over, which meant my real reason for being there could begin. We could get to the after-sport socialising, i.e., the whole point of sport, as far as I was concerned.

'So,' I said, as Reeta and I rolled up our mats. 'Where shall we go now?

'Home?' she said with a shrug.

'No!' I said, 'That's not the idea at all! I've come all this way and done all this sport now. We have to do something! That's the whole point, Reets!'

'Is it?'

I turned to the girl I'd been next to, who I'd tried – and failed – to engage in conversation. She was pulling on a hoody and re-tying her hair. I knew it was rather forward to approach her now, but what choice did I have? If I didn't make a move, I might never see her again.

'Shall we go for a cup of tea?' I said to her.

'Sorry?' she said. She looked genuinely alarmed.

'Would you like a cup of tea?' I said again.

She looked down at my hands, as if I might be holding the tea as I spoke.

'No,' she said. And then, as if remembering her manners. 'I mean, no thank you. Sorry. I've got to get home. I've got work tomorrow so stuff to do . . .' She trailed off.

'Oh, OK,' I said, trying to sound bright, despite my disappointment. 'See you next week then, maybe?'

'Maybe,' she said, but I could tell from her voice that she was hoping I wouldn't come along next week at all.

Don't worry, I wanted to tell her, I don't think I will.

The Secret's Out

When I arrived at college the next day, I found Til pacing up and down outside the front gates talking into her phone. Every so often she was stopping and throwing her free hand up in the air in an exasperated kind of way.

As I approached her, she ended the call and shoved her phone in her pocket.

'What's the matter?'

'Lady Gaga.'

'The dog one?'

'Yeah.'

I could tell she was stressed then because her usual style would have been to say something sarcastic and annoying like 'obviously' or 'no, the singer, I just really hate her work'.

'What's the matter with her?'

She started walking fast into college so I walked alongside her, dodging past other students to keep up.

'She's been found out.'

I was confused. 'What do you mean? What was her secret?'

'No secret. I just mean that she's a dog. A big dog in our flat.'

I grabbed Til's arm to get her to slow down. 'What? What did they think she was? Did your mum not realise she was a dog . . . ? Did she think she was a bear too?' It was an easy mistake to make, after all.

'What I mean,' Til said, stopping in front of me, 'is that someone has told the landlord that we've got Lady Gaga. As in, we've got a massive big hairy dog in our flat when we're not allowed one.'

'Oh,' I said. 'I see. Did your mum not know you weren't allowed?'

Til rolled her eyes. 'She knew. She's just a dope and never thinks anything through.'

'So what are you going to do? Will Lady Gaga have to go back?'

'There's nowhere for her to go back to. We could re-home her – we should re-home her – but Mum won't. She says she loves her too much.'

'So what will you do?'

'Move.'

'Really? You have to move out?'

Til nodded and rested her head against her locker. It really wasn't like her to be this stressy.

'Can't you . . .' I paused. I knew from experience that trying to be helpful when Til was annoyed was only likely to make her more annoyed. 'Can't you persuade your mum that there's a better place for Lady Gaga? And maybe she can . . . visit?'

Til chewed on her bottom lip. 'I dunno. The thing is, she has been a lot happier since we got her. Like, god knows why because she's a nightmare, but Mum really loves her and she likes having someone to look after. In a way, I think it would be easier to get a new flat. Maybe a little house with a garden.'

'Oh, OK,' I said. 'Well, that sounds like a good plan?'

'Easier said than done though.' Til sighed. 'Landlords aren't exactly thrilled at the idea of having a huge dribbly dog jumping around the place.'

I nodded. 'Yeah. How long have you got?'

'Four weeks.'

She closed her locker and walked quickly down the corridor without waiting to see if I was coming.

Fire

At lunchtime, I found my usual seat in the canteen and took out my field study notebook.

As I wrote the date at the top of a new page I noticed that it was nearly two weeks since the American diner party and my realisation that I was in danger of turning into someone whose only friend was a pork pie, and I wasn't sure I'd made much – any – progress in that time. I decided to write some notes to recap where I was:

Hypothesis 1: Getting noticed is the key
Findings: While relatively easy to attract attention, converting attention into meaningful interaction is far more complex and needs further consideration. Also noted that alarming appearance may actively discourage conversation.

Hypothesis 2: Sports are a great way to meet people
Findings: Hypothesis only holds true for people with genuine interest in sport. (I.e., not me.)

Hypothesis 3: Activity first, friends later. Just join anything.
Findings: Dangerous approach to be attempted only by those with advanced social skills (i.e., not me).

The problems with my approaches so far had been easy to see, but what wasn't so easy was working out what to do about it.

Once again, I started to wonder if it was just all completely random, and that whether you got to live your life as one of the charmed chosen ones, loved by everyone and invited to everything, was a matter of complete luck. It was like photos on Instagram that seemed to have a crazy number of likes for no particular reason, or singers who had thousands and thousands of fans even though they sounded very similar to all the others: once someone started to become popular – once something was seen to be liked – then more people wanted to like it too.

I was pleased with this observation, although I had no idea what to do with it. I added a note to the bottom of my page:

Popularity breeds popularity

I underlined it three times.

I looked over at the Booth, where Luke was sitting with his feet up on a table and Kendall was weaving tiny plaits into his floppy curly hair. I couldn't remember a time when they hadn't been at the top of the social order, admired by everyone, but it must have started somewhere. What did they do first? Who did they have to impress?

Just then, a loud horn sounded, jolting me out of my thoughts, and the red light on the wall above the vending machine began to flash manically. People stopped their conversations and looked round.

The fire alarm.

Some people put their hands over their ears or pulled their hoods up to hide from the sound, but others turned back to their conversations and tried to ignore it, assuming that it was a false alarm and hoping that someone would shut the stupid thing up.

When a full minute went by without any signs of the noise stopping, people began looking up at the flashing light anxiously.

'We don't need to actually go outside, do we?' one girl called to her friend above the noise. 'It's freezing.'

Her question was answered when Leroy, my psychology tutor, came through the double doors, strode into the middle of the room and clapped his hands. 'Right, everyone out, please! You know where to go. Leave your stuff where it is. Nice and orderly, no pushing.'

Reluctantly, people began to get to their feet. Everyone ignored his instructions about the stuff and began shoving phones and books and half-eaten sandwiches into their bags and pulling on coats and hoodies. People shuffled out of the glass doors labelled Fire Exit with as much enthusiasm as you'd imagine when it's raining outside and you're sure the alarm is only going off because someone in the tech room has got carried away with a soldering iron.

I put my notebook back in my bag, zipped up my coat and followed the others outside.

As soon as I stepped through the glass doors and onto the field I could tell something was wrong. In the canteen we'd been cushioned by the warm chip-fat cloud; outside, a new smell hit: it was a bitter, chemically smell. Barbecue sauce mixed with burning rubber.

'What's the smell?' people were saying to each other. 'It must be a real fire?'

And then someone said, 'Oh my god, look!', and when we looked where other people were looking, across the field and around the back of college, we could see the thick black smoke, rising in a slow but steady plume.

It was coming from Mac's cottage.

Mac and Mrs Mac

'Mac!' people began to say to each other, eyes wide in fear and shock. 'Mac's cottage is on fire! Where is he? Where's Mrs Mac? Are they inside?'

'We've got to do something!' one girl called. 'We've got to get them out!'

'Everyone go to the assembly point!' Leroy called, clapping his hands together again. 'Do not go any nearer! The fire brigade is on its way!'

And just a few seconds later, we heard loud sirens and saw two fire engines pull up at the front of college. I did as I was told and headed to the area along the edge of the fence where we had to queue in our tutor groups to be counted, but I kept looking over towards the cottage. The firemen had jumped out and were unwinding huge yellow hoses from the back of their trucks.

I thought about Mac. I'd only been talking to him a few hours earlier when he was repairing a loose corner of carpet in my business studies classroom and I'd almost walked into him. As usual, he'd asked me how my day was going and when I returned the question, he'd said, 'Great! A belter today, actually. Had to come in at seven to fix a leak in the gents.'

'Oh,' I said. 'Is that . . . good?'

'You betcha! Early starts mean breakfast in the canteen. Sausage, eggs and beans, would you believe! Mrs Mac wouldn't have me cooking that at home. "Do you think I want to go to work smelling of sausage!" is what she always says.'

Where had Mac gone after he'd finishing fixing the carpet, I wondered. Had he stayed in college or had he headed home for lunch? I very much hoped there had been something in urgent need of his attention that had kept him in college and away from home. And that Mrs Mac was somewhere safe too.

According to the drill we'd all practised in the first week of the new term, we were supposed to stand in a line next to the plastic numbered signs representing our tutor groups, which were tied onto the fence, but no one was really sticking to the rules. Even the tutors were wandering around looking shocked and concerned and like they weren't quite sure what to be doing.

After fifteen minutes or so, although the air was still foggy, the smoke no longer seemed to be rising in such a steady stream. A fireman walked over and said something to one of the tutors, who nodded seriously, then called the other tutors over into a little team huddle. Then Leroy came back to report the news.

'OK, folks, we've had the all-clear that we're fine to go

back inside. The fire was contained to the cottage so the main college is perfectly safe.'

'What about Mac?' Martin called. 'Is he OK?'

Leroy shrugged helplessly. 'I've heard nothing to say he isn't. So I suggest we presume everything's fine.'

But no one was satisfied with that answer and as we all shuffled back inside and made our way to our afternoon classes, theories and rumours began to spread. Had the cottage been struck by lightning? Had the fire been started deliberately? In revenge for some substandard repairs done by Mac? Had they made us all come inside so they could remove Mac's and Mrs Mac's bodies without us seeing?

At three o'clock, we were called to the main hall. We made our way there in a hushed silence, everyone sure we were being summoned to hear the worst. So, when we were all assembled and out from behind the curtain stepped none other than Mac himself, a huge cheer went up, and people began hugging and wiping their eyes in relief.

When Mac had waved his hand to quieten everyone down, he said, 'Sorry, everyone, for the fuss. Didn't mean to cause a drama. All it was, was that we had a power cut this morning when I got up, so I had to light a candle and have a shave over a bowl in the kitchen. Like something out of Victorian times, it was! But anyway, silly old me left the blummin' candle out, didn't I. Next thing, I'm having my cuppa looking out the window in the art room and blow me down if the whole place isn't on fire. Now Mrs Mac's got the right old hump as you can imagine!' He grinned down at us from the stage, like he found the whole episode thoroughly amusing. 'Still, it's like I said to her: we'd been putting off painting that kitchen for months – now we won't have to bother!'

It was exactly typical of Mac to be so cheery about the whole thing and it was a big relief to everyone to see him not only alive and well, but not too worried about the fact that his whole house had just burnt down.

Back in afternoon classes, Mac was still the main topic of conversation.

'Apparently he lost everything,' Martin said.

'Everything?' someone asked.

Our tutor, Piers, nodded to confirm this. 'It does look that way. Poor guy didn't have contents insurance.'

'What does that mean?' Reeta asked.

'It means that the insurance company will pay for the bricks and mortar, for the cottage to be repaired, but for all his stuff inside – clothes, TV, phone, computer, books, everything – he'll get nothing. It's just gone.'

'Oh my god, I would literally die if my phone got burnt,' Molly Shaw said.

'Well,' Piers said, 'obviously Mac, and everyone, is just glad that . . . that it wasn't worse. But still, to be left with nothing is a pretty rough hand to be dealt.'

A Favour

When I got home I heard Mum calling me from her bedroom, where, aside from trips to the bathroom aided by me, Ollie or Dad, she had been lying flat on her back, looking at the ceiling since her back had given way over a week earlier.

'Grace! Can you come up here?'

'How's it going?' I said, going into her room. 'Do you need something?'

'I'm just so *bored*, really,' Mum said. 'Dad's getting me a tea. But, I wanted to ask you a favour. It's about Paddy's birthday.'

'I thought you'd already got him all the plastic junk he could ever need off the internet? You need me to get anything from town?'

'No, I think we're all right for plastic junk. It's more his party I'm thinking about.'

'He's having a party?'

Mum nodded and winced. I wasn't sure if that was because of her bad back or the thought of fifteen small wild children tearing around the house. 'Tomorrow.'

I shuddered. 'I guess I'd better ask Til if I can take shelter round hers then.'

'Well, that's the thing,' Mum said.

'What's the thing?'

'Dad's been asked to do an extra shift at work.'

I realised immediately where this was going.

'Oh no,' I said, physically backing away from Mum. 'No way. I'm just going to stop you right there. Kids' birthday parties are well outside of my remit.'

'Oh, come on, Grace,' Mum wheedled. 'I can barely even sit upright. There's no way I can serve jelly and ice cream and play host to a tank of lizards.'

'What? What lizards?'

'I've booked Mr Lizard to come and entertain them all. Have you heard of him? I read about him online and thought Paddy would love him.'

'Who – and in fact, what – on earth is Mr Lizard?'

'Mr Lizard is a man. A man with a beard and a sort of explorer-type waistcoat. But he brings with him a whole tank of lizards for the kids to look at. They can touch some of them too. Kids love it apparently, keeps them occupied for ages. And you know how into his reptiles Paddy is at the moment. So you wouldn't need to do much, just be on hand for general supervision and wiping up spillages. Mr Lizard will take care of the actual entertaining.'

I made a face. 'That is such a gross idea. What if they escape? What if we're finding tiny lizards swimming in the toilet for weeks to come?'

Mum sighed and shifted her position on her pillow. 'I'm

sure he's got all the appropriate security precautions in place.'

I groaned and sat down heavily on the end of Mum's bed, making her wince again. 'Why did you tell Paddy he could have a party in the first place? He wouldn't even know it was his birthday if you hadn't told him! Let's just tell him it's cancelled. Or that it's already happened! He never knows what's real and what's not. We'll just say he already had his party last weekend and that he had a lovely time. He'll believe us if we say it enough times.'

'Grace, we've sent all the invites,' Mum said. 'And we can't let all the other parents down. They'll have been counting on it as a way to get their kids out of the house for an afternoon. That's the way these things work – hosting one party means invites to ten others, which means ten afternoons of free babysitting. We have to take our turn.'

'Oh great,' I said, standing up again. 'So I have to give up my Saturday afternoon to be an unpaid children's entertainer. A nanny. A clown!'

'I've bought the food online already so that'll be arriving first thing. So it's just a case of letting Mr Lizard in and then making sure the kids don't chew on the furniture or set fire to the curtains.'

I didn't say anything.

'Please, Grace?' Mum said.

She looked exhausted just thinking about it. I knew I couldn't say no.

'OK, OK. Fine.'

Mr Lizard

At eight the next morning, I was woken up when my phone began to buzz on my bedside table. I picked it up and looked at the screen. It was Mum.

'Mum?' I said groggily into the handset. 'Why are you calling? Where are you?'

'Just in my room. Could you come in here please?'

Mum sounded so serious that I hung up the call immediately, threw off my duvet and dashed across the landing to her bedroom.

'What is it?' I said as I burst through the door. 'Have you fallen out of bed?'

'What? No?' Mum said, from her position, clearly still very much in bed. Dad had already left for work. A half-drunk mug of tea was on his bedside table.

'What's happened then?'

'Well, the thing is . . .' Mum began carefully. 'It's about Mr Lizard.'

'What about him?'

'He's not coming.'

'Not coming where? Here? To the party? Why?'

Mum frowned. 'Not sure entirely. I couldn't really hear his voicemail. Something to do with a lizard that he thought was a boy turning out to be a girl . . . it's caused all sorts of cohabitation complications that he needs to sort out, apparently.'

'Right,' I said. I wasn't really ready to think about who exactly lizards did and didn't like to live with when I had been awake less than five minutes. 'So what about the party? Shall we postpone?'

Mum shook her head. 'We can't. We really can't. I've bought all the food and everyone's expecting it. We'll just have to improvise.'

'We?' I said, raising one eyebrow.

'I've made you a list,' Mum said, reaching for the notepad on her bedside table and passing it to me. 'There's plenty on there to keep them occupied. The time will fly by!'

I looked down at the paper.

Musical Statues
Musical Bumps
Pass the Parcel
Sleeping Lions
Pin the Tail on the Donkey
Musical Chairs
Duck Duck Goose

'What parcel are they supposed to pass? Do we have a parcel?'

'Oh, just get them to pass a cushion,' Mum said. 'They won't notice the difference. Give them a sweet when the music stops.'

Mum seemed to be very casual about swindling a bunch of children but then she was going to be safely tucked away up here. I was the one expected to appear on the front line.

'*Mum*,' I groaned. 'It'll be impossible to get them to play these properly. Three-year-olds are practically babies.'

'Oh, they're mostly not three,' Mum said. 'One or two little ones from nursery but then it's brothers and sisters too, so I think the average age will be nearer six.'

'Wonderful. Practically adults. Why don't we have a dinner party instead.'

'It'll be fine,' Mum said. 'It doesn't matter if they follow the rules to the letter, as long as they're busy. Play Sleeping Lions if you need a rest, then they'll all just lie quietly on the floor. They might even doze off if you're lucky.'

'OK,' I breathed out heavily. 'I can see I don't have any choice. But I'm really not looking forward to it.'

'The food's arriving at ten. If you can just, you know, lay it out. Make it look like a party.'

'Fine. Whatever.' I took Mum's list and I went and got back into bed to get some rest while I had the chance.

Lizard Party

Ollie was away at a paintballing weekend for one of his friend's brother's twenty-first birthday. When he'd told me about it, I'd said I couldn't think of anything worse than spending a whole day running around in freezing mud having people jump out from behind trees to point a gun at me, but that was before I'd had to consider the prospect of two hours with fifteen hyped-up children, armed with nothing but a scribbled list of old-fashioned games.

I texted both Til and Reeta to see if they would come over for moral and practical support, but Til said she was taking Lady Gaga for a big long walk to try to run off some energy and Reeta had a running club meet.

I sat on the edge of the bed, looking at the wall. This, I thought, was a prime example of why I needed to work on my popularity. If I had more friends, more than two (or one and a half, if you considered that Til found me annoying most of the time) then statistically speaking, my chances of finding someone willing to help me when I needed it would go right up. It wasn't just good for one's self-esteem to be popular; it was more convenient.

Just then, Paddy ran into my room pulling Dustbin the

lizard along by his back leg.

'Gracie, is it my lizard party yet?'

'Not yet,' I said.

'Mr Lizard, Mr Lizard, Mr Lizard! Paddy shouted, waving Dustbin around his head.

Great, I thought. I hadn't realised Mum had told him specifically about Mr Lizard – and that he'd remember it.

'The thing is, buddy . . .' I began.

Paddy looked at me expectantly. I hesitated, but I decided if he was going to have a meltdown about it I'd rather get it out the way nice and early before the other children arrived. 'The thing is . . .' I said again, 'is that Mr Lizard won't be able to come today after all.'

Paddy froze and look at me wide-eyed. 'Mr Lizard?'

I nodded. 'It's just that he realised that the lizards had another appointment to go to. At the . . . dentist. So they can't come here today. But they asked me to pass on the message that they hope you have a really great birthday.'

'No lizards?' His eyes were brimming with tears. Oh god. This was worse than a meltdown.

'No lizards,' I said quietly.

The tears began to spill over and fall silently down his cheeks. 'No lizard party.'

I pulled him onto my lap. 'Oh no, we are absolutely going to have a lizard party. We don't need Mr Lizard! You'll be there, and Dustbin will be there, and all your friends! And we'll have lizard games and lizard foods.'

He hiccupped and looked up at me. 'What's lizard foods?'

'You'll just have to wait and see!'

A Little Bread Snake

As soon as the food delivery Mum had ordered arrived, I carted it from the hall to the kitchen and unloaded it all on the kitchen table.

'Right then, Paddywhack, you ready to make some lizard food?'

'Yeah!' he shouted, pumping both fists in the air.

Even as I said it, I still didn't know exactly what we were going to do, so I decided we'd just have to get started and hope for the best.

An hour later, I was so proud of my handiwork I took a photo on my phone and went up to show Mum in bed.

'Check this out, Mum,' I said. 'Have you ever seen so much reptile- and amphibian- themed food in your life?'

Mum squinted at the screen, zooming in to explore the banquet I'd laid out on the dining-room table.

'Oh, cute,' she said. 'A little bread snake.'

I had lined all of the round rolls, filled with cheese and egg, up into a wiggly row, with two raisin eyes and a little red tongue fashioned out of apple peel on the one at the front.

'Yep,' I said proudly. 'We've also got lizards' tongues, crocodiles' eggs and frog pops. And a swamp.' I pointed in turn to the strawberry ribbons I'd sliced into the shape of tongues, hard-boiled eggs I'd rolled in crisp crumbs for texture, cake pops I'd covered in green icing and cut a slit for a mouth. The swamp was the bowl of standard lime jelly Dad had already prepared, but I'd made Paddy go and find one of the packets of jelly snakes he always had lying around his room and poked them into it to give the kids an extra surprise when they put their faces in it.

'Well done, darling,' Mum said. 'I'm sure Paddy's delighted.'

Paddy did indeed seem happier than he had been when I'd had to break the news of Mr Lizard's cancellation to him, and was at that moment sitting in the kitchen looking out over the display with his hands tucked under his bum like he didn't trust himself not to grab it all and rub it on his face. I only hoped he was going to stay happy when the other children arrived and I was left to entertain them for two hours.

The first time the doorbell went was at 2.50 p.m. – a full ten minutes before the official start time but I didn't think I could really ask them to wait in the drive. Instead, I helped the small boy who was delivered into my care climb out of his coat and shoes and ushered him in the lounge.

By five past three, everyone was assembled.

To begin with, everything went well. Better than I'd expected at least. My plan was to follow Mum's list but, to make up for the Mr Lizard disappointment, add an extra reptilian twist wherever possible.

'Musical statues! When the music stops, pretend to be a lizard!'

'Musical bumps now! Dance like a lizard until you sit down!'

'It's time to be sleeping lizards now, everyone!'

The only problem was, it turned out that when they wanted to, small children could work quickly. By four fifteen we'd played all the games on Mum's list, they'd demolished the lizard tea and there were still forty-five minutes to fill before I could hand them back to their parents.

'What will we do now?' a girl of about five called Evelyn asked me.

'Hide-and-seek!' shouted her little brother Louis, clambering over the sofa and dropping – alarmingly – headfirst down the back.

I quickly realised that fifteen children tearing around the house opening cupboards and emptying bins in search of hiding places would be a sure-fire way to lose control of proceedings, but luckily Evelyn wasn't happy to accept her younger brother's decision anyway.

'You can't choose,' she told him crossly. 'The grown-up has to choose.'

Fifteen jelly-smeared, hopeful faces looked up at me.

'Oh, I'm not a grown-up,' I told her, feigning surprise at the very idea. 'I'm a kid, just like you. I'm only four years old.'

Evelyn looked at me, her eyes narrowed. 'No, you're not. You're big.'

I wasn't sure where the idea had come from, or where it was going, but I carried on regardless. 'Oh,' I said casually.

'I'm just really, really tall for my age. But I am really only four. How old are you?'

'Five,' she said.

'See! I'm even younger than you.'

She frowned, thinking about this.

'In fact,' I said to the sea of faces. 'I've been meaning to tell you. The thing is – the big secret –' I lowered my voice to a stage whisper – 'Is that there are no grown-ups here *at all*.'

One girl gasped. The others just gazed at me, fascinated.

'So that means – and I'm really hoping you'll be able to help me out here – that we need to be the grown-ups.'

There was a stunned silence for a moment. Then Evelyn said, 'What does that *mean*?'

I shrugged. 'I don't know. But someone's got to do it. What do grown-ups even do all day? Does anyone know?'

'Drive!' a boy shouted, jumping up and down in excitement. 'They drive cars and ice-cream vans!'

'Yes!' I said. 'You're right! Can you drive the ice-cream van for us, please?' I directed him to the armchair in the corner. 'Climb on the seat. That's right. Then hold the wheel.'

The boy put his hands on the imaginary wheel and pretended to steer.

'That's right!' I said. 'Who needs grown-ups? We've got an ice-cream van! Remember to stop and make an ice cream for anyone who wants one.'

The kids began to get into the game, shouting out their ideas for what we needed to be doing if we were going to properly take care of things in the grown-ups' absence.

'We need to talk on the telephone all day!'

'We need to hang out the washing on the line!'

'We need to drink all the wine in the big wine glasses then dance around the kitchen like this.' One small girl began to wobble around the living room with her eyes half closed. 'Then we need to say "just give me some space, Steven!" and fall asleep in a chair.'

'OK!' I said, I decided it was better to take her word for it and not to ask too many questions about where she'd got the idea from, or indeed who Steven was.

One by one, each of the children began acting out what they thought they should be doing if they were to take their responsibilities seriously.

Paddy decided that it was important, if we were really grown-ups, that we should all be wearing grown-up make-up, so I went and fetched his face paints for him and sat patiently on a chair while he used the red stick to paint my lips and cheeks and the blue one to give me eye shadow all the way up my forehead.

At five o'clock on the dot the doorbell rang, signalling that my duties were approaching their end. When I went to open the door, I was alarmed to find Molly Shaw, of the Booth fame, standing on the step. I immediately wished my forehead wasn't painted bright blue and that I didn't have a dribble of green jelly running down my front.

'Oh,' I said. 'Hi. Molly?'

She seemed as surprised to see me as I was her. 'Oh yeah, hi. I don't know if I've got the right house? I'm here to pick up my niece and nephew. Evelyn and Louis? You're from my college, aren't you?'

I nodded. 'Yeah. That's right. And yeah, you've got the right place. They're here. Paddy is my little brother. It's his party. Come in.'

I stood aside to let Molly battle her way through the porch packed with small coats and trainers, and led her through to the lounge, where the children were still seriously going about their adult business.

'Auntie Molly!' Evelyn cried when she saw her, and wrapped her arms around Molly's waist.

Molly laughed. 'Hello, trouble. You had fun?'

To my relief, Evelyn nodded enthusiastically and began to explain what each of the partygoers was responsible for. 'It's not always easy to be in charge,' she explained seriously. 'But someone's got to do it.' With this last sentence, she shook her head and held out her palms in a comically exaggerated gesture of adult weariness.

Molly laughed again and said, 'Cool game.'

I shrugged. 'I had to think on my feet.'

As Evelyn went to collect the party bags I had laid out for her and her brother on the side in the kitchen, I gave Molly a quick run-down of the events of the day, covering the no-show of Mr Lizard, the improvisation of the lizard games and the hastily – although, I had to say, inspired – assembly of the lizard tea.

'Wow,' Molly said. She seemed genuinely impressed. 'I don't know how you managed to think of it all.'

I shrugged. 'Didn't have much choice, I guess.'

'Seriously,' she said, picking up a leftover frog-pop from the table and examining it. 'I make cakes sometimes – like birthday cakes for parties and that – but just a cake takes us, like, weeks to plan.'

'For the kids?' I said, nodding towards Evelyn, who was holding onto Molly's leg, her thumb in her mouth.

'Well, yeah,' Molly said. 'But for anyone really. Anyone who needs one. I mean, they pay. It's like this business thing we run.

'Oh cool,' I said. 'That sounds good. I'd love to do something like that.'

I didn't know if that last part was true but it did sound impressive and I did badly want the conversation – my first real one with someone from the Booth – to go well.

Once Evelyn and Louis were bundled up into their coats and we were in the porch, ready to say goodbye, Molly turned to me and said, 'You know we were talking, actually, about getting someone.'

'Sorry?'

'Our business – Bashed, it's called – we do cakes, like I said, and a few times we've done a bit of other food, like . . . we did a quiche once.' She paused and looked off into the distance for a moment like she was remembering the quiche fondly. 'But sometimes people want more. Like a full party service. And me and Kendall were saying –'

'Kendall?' I couldn't stop myself from blurting out.

'Yeah, Kendall Cross. She's at our college too, do you know her? It was her thing originally, the business. She set it up last year. Then I joined. Anyway, we were saying that it would be good to expand. Because some people want more than the cake. They want, like, someone to take the whole thing off their hands. Entertainment and that. You know?'

'Oh,' I said nodding. 'Yeah.' Although I wasn't quite sure I did.

'So if you're interested, I can ask Kendall? If you want to see how it goes?'

I honestly had no real idea what it was she thought I was interested in or what I would be joining, but the idea of Molly talking to Kendall about me was too exciting to overlook. 'Oh yeah, definitely,' I said, nodding earnestly again. 'I'd definitely be up for that.'

'Cool.' Molly smiled. 'I'll talk to Kendall and message you later.'

'OK,' I said. 'Great.'

I still wasn't sure what the message would say, but I was very much looking forward to its arrival.

At eight-thirty that evening, when I'd crawled into bed and turned out all the lights, completely exhausted by my afternoon of hosting, the message came through:

Hey Grace, Kendall is totally psyched by the idea of you doing the entertainments for Bashed but we'll need to see if it's a good match. Come over to Kendall's tomorrow at about 7 and we can talk.

She signed off with Kendall's address and three kisses.

Well, I thought, lying back and looking at the glow in the dark stars on my ceiling. Three kisses and a personal invitation from a member of the Booth.

This was *not* how I expected the day to end.

PART 3:

Where I reinvent myself as an entertainer, investigator and philanthropist

An Interview

As soon as I woke up the next day I remembered something important was due to happen, but it took a few moments for me to actually remember my appointment at Kendall's.

Was that what it was? It sounded so serious, so professional. I still wasn't sure exactly what it would entail or what the outcome might be, but whatever it was, it was beyond exciting to have been invited – summoned? – to Kendall's house.

I couldn't stop thinking about how until now if we'd walked past each other in college, Kendall wouldn't have even stopped to say hello. I knew who she was only because she was so pretty and carefree and sophisticated-looking. She probably didn't even know my name. Or at least, hadn't last week. But now she and Molly had had a conversation about me and here I was, getting ready to go right into her actual house.

I wanted to find out a bit more about what we might be talking about, so I searched for Bashed online. It didn't take me long to find their website.

Bashed Events Ltd: Stunning cakes and more!

I clicked on the 'About us' link.

**Founded by Eddie Cruz and Kendall Cross
Cakes AND MORE for all occasions**

See our gallery for a selection of our work

I had never given much thought to cake decorating before, but the pictures in the gallery were amazing. They didn't even look like cakes. They looked like sculptures. Like works of art. There were cakes shaped like ponds with icing so clear and shiny I couldn't see how it wasn't real water, with little icing ducks floating on the top. There was a cake in the form of an enormous hamburger, complete with polystyrene box. There was a cake that seemed to defy gravity, with a Smarties tube suspended in the air and a cascade of Smarties raining down on it.

At the bottom, there were some pictures of what I supposed they meant by 'And more' – themed buffets that put mine to shame. One that particularly caught my eye was something that looked like an ordinary roast dinner but, on reading the notes I was told that the beef joint was really a chocolate cake, the Yorkshire puddings were sweet batter filled with toffee sauce and the Brussels sprouts were chocolate truffles wrapped in pistachio icing. It was all quite brilliant. But it really got me no nearer to answering the question of what exactly they wanted me for.

I studied Molly's message, looking for clues as to what they had in mind.

'To see if it's a good match,' she'd said. What exactly might I be a good match for?

Still, whatever it was, it seemed clear to me this was some kind of interview. And that, as I saw it, was a good thing, because one thing I liked was preparing for interviews.

When I was younger I used to spend a lot of time fantasising about going to job interviews in the same way other kids dreamt about big white weddings or playing football for their favourite team. For some reason, to nine-year-old me, it was the part of being grown up that seemed most glamorous.

I would do both sides of the conversation, setting myself interesting, probing questions, and then practise what I'd say, right down to the body language and the (of, course) made-up examples of past work I would share.

In fact, I'd been incredibly disappointed when the time came for my first real interview – our work experience placements in Year Ten – and I'd gone to meet the boss of a local advertising agency, armed with a file of pictures cut out from magazines and notes on what I thought made an effective marketing campaign as well as a detailed script explaining why I felt I had what it takes to make it big in the cut-throat world of digital advertising, and he hadn't asked to look at any of it. He'd simply given me the briefest of smiles and asked me to empty the paper recycling bins.

Anyway, although I wasn't exactly sure what Kendall would be looking for in me, I wasn't about to let this opportunity to infiltrate her inner circle pass me by through lack of preparation.

'Someone to take the whole thing off their hands', 'Entertainment' – that's what Molly had said. I could work with that.

Luckily, we were quiet at Podrick's that day, so I was able to spend the majority of my seven-hour shift with my eyes glued to my phone searching for anything and everything I could think of to do with party planning:

Great party ideas

How to make your party go with a bang

Stun your guests with these party themes they'd never expect

I thought the best plan was to cover as many angles as possible, to maximise my chances of being able to appear flexible and unfazed by whatever they might suggest.

That evening, I arrived at Kendall's road twenty-five minutes earlier than I'd intended because I'd got an early bus to allow for mishaps – the last thing I wanted was to turn up late and look like I didn't care – but then there weren't any mishaps, so I had to walk around the block to kill some time.

As I was doing my second loop and walking away from Kendall's house, I saw a figure coming towards me. I realised it was Molly and it was too late to pretend I hadn't seen her.

'Oh, hi, Grace,' she said. 'You know . . . you're going the wrong way? It's down the road?'

I looked behind me and feigned surprise. 'Oh! Oh is it? I'm hopeless with directions, always getting lost!'

It had been my automatic reaction. It seemed preferable, for some reason, to pretend I was just a bit ditzy and clueless, rather than to admit how excited I was about the meeting. But as soon as I said it, I realised that this wasn't a good first impression to give. This wasn't just a social call. It was an interview! And I could imagine that planning parties would involve quite a lot of going to people's houses and those people wouldn't be too pleased if I was turning up late because I was hopeless with directions.

'I mean,' I added quickly. 'I did know where Kendall's house was. I was just having a quick look around first. To check out the area.'

Molly frowned. 'OK. And it's OK with you, is it? The area?'

I nodded enthusiastically. 'Yes. Yes, lovely.'

'Shall we . . . go . . . then?'

'Yes!' I nodded enthusiastically. 'Yes, let's go.'

Kendall's house was big with a front garden bigger than my front and back garden put together. There were two old cars in the driveway. I didn't know enough about cars to know exactly what type they were, but they looked cool and old-fashioned – the kind you might see people in films driving along the sea front with a picnic hamper on the back seat.

I was surprised when Molly just pushed the front door open without ringing the doorbell, but I followed her in.

Kendall's room was up two flights of stairs in the converted attic of the house. Once again, Molly walked right in without knocking.

Kendall was sitting at her desk, typing quickly on her laptop.

'Hey, babe,' Molly said, giving Kendall an air kiss. Then she settled down on Kendall's bed, lay back on the pillow and started looking at her phone.

I hovered awkwardly in the doorway. I'd never even really spoken to Kendall before. Not even in passing. Not even to say, for example, 'Is this seat taken?' So definitely not in a situation where she was actively looking for my input into a conversation.

At first, Kendall carried on typing and didn't acknowledge me at all. I wondered if she even realised I was standing there. I was just wondering whether I should cough or say 'Hello!' to get her attention when, all of a sudden, she stopped typing, spun her chair around and said, 'Grace!' as if I'd just that moment appeared and the whole thing was a total surprise for her.

'Hi!' I said, my voice coming out strangely and sounding a bit like a little horn.

She stood up and took hold of me by my upper arms, peering at me like a mother might inspect their child's face for dirt. 'So!' she said. 'Molly says you want to join Bashed.'

'Yeah!' I said. It seemed rude to contradict her but I wasn't sure I had ever said that to Molly exactly.

'OK!' Kendall said, picking up a plastic folding chair and opening it out in the middle of her room. 'Let's see if you're going to be suitable to get on board.'

'Sure,' I said. 'Sounds good.'

She gestured to a chair. 'Sit, sit.'

I did as I was told and she and Molly perched on the edge of the bed, facing me.

I felt very on-show suddenly. It really was like an interview. Or perhaps a quiz show. I half expected a spotlight to come on over my head.

'Right. So,' Kendall said. 'Tell us about you.'

'Well,' I said. 'I live with my parents and my brothers. I go to Coniston. But I mean, obviously you know that!' I laughed, just to try and lighten the mood a little, but they didn't even smile. They continued peering at me. 'I'm doing art, psychology and business studies. I –'

Kendall held up her hand to stop me. 'Grace,' she said, with a smile 'We don't want your CV. Time is money. We need the good stuff.'

'Good stuff . . .' I said. What good stuff? 'Oh OK,' I said, like I knew exactly what she meant. 'Well, when I was three I ate a tiny plastic skeleton and my parents had to rush me to hospital and we've still got the X-ray picture of it just sitting in my stomach. Minus one arm, which I must have chewed off.'

Kendall frowned very slightly, and they looked at each other, then back at me. 'I mean,' Kendall said slowly, her voice suddenly bright and sing-song like she was talking to a child or an idiot, 'your ideas. Your experience.'

I laughed as if there had been a hilarious misunderstanding. 'Oh, I see! Yeah, of course. Well –'

'OK,' Kendall said, suddenly getting to her feet. 'Let's

do it the other way around. We'll talk. You listen. Then we'll swap.'

I blinked, surprised by the sudden change of tack. 'Yep. OK. Sure.'

Kendall went to the corner of her room and stood with her hands in the pockets of her dress. 'OK, so our business was founded by my boyfriend Eddie two years ago as an assignment in his business class.'

'Oh, I take business too, actually. I –'

Kendall held up her hand to quieten me. 'Yeah, you said, babe. That's great.' She gave me a patient smile like I'd just told her about the ten-metre swimming badge I'd got when I was six. 'So, as I was saying, my boyfriend, Eddie –'

'Now ex-boyfriend,' Molly cut in.

Kendall shot her a look. 'Well, yeah, but he was my boyfriend at the time.'

'He's in Scotland now,' Molly said. 'For uni.'

Kendall explained that when Eddie was doing his A levels he'd been tasked with setting up a fictional small business and had come up with the idea of a company that provided bespoke decorated cakes for occasions.

'Because I've always been into doing cakes,' Kendall explained. 'So that's what gave him the idea in the first place.'

She told me that originally, the assignment had been entirely hypothetical – an exercise in drawing up a theoretical business plan – but when the assignment was finished, he realised he could make it work for real.

'Eddie did the set-up – he made the website and did the advertising and everything. But I did the cakes. Now I've

102

trained Molly up, she does more of the hands-on stuff, but I'm the mastermind. If you know what I mean.'

I didn't quite, but I nodded anyway. 'But Eddie isn't involved now?'

Kendall shook her head quickly. 'No.' She pulled what looked like a long pencil out of her hair and shook it down so it fell over her face. 'We broke up. And he didn't have time to do the business any more anyway. So now I do it. And just recently, we've started branching out. Creating interesting, innovative party food for our clients. You know what innovative means?'

'Yeah. It –'

'It means new. Inventive,' Kendall said.

'Like what you did for your brother,' said Molly.

'Yeah!' Kendall said, suddenly smiling widely. 'Molly told me about the tongues and the feet and the swamp and everything. That sounded cool, Grace. You know, new? That's what we're talking about!'

I felt myself glow at this sudden praise after the brisk start to things. 'Oh, well, I've got loads of ideas for that kind of thing,' I said, picking up my bag to take out the notes I had been taking as I carried out my research. 'For example, I was thinking the other day how I'd like to create a whole campsite out of food. Does that sound mad? But you know, a little campfire made out of chilli so it's really "fiery" and –'

Kendall waved her hand. 'Let's get to all that in a minute.'

'Oh,' I said. 'OK.'

'To be honest, Grace, it wasn't really the food we wanted you for. I was more interested in what you had the kids doing. Molly told me how you were commanding the event!'

103

'Was I?' I looked at Molly, who nodded seriously.

Kendall went on to explain how Bashed was 'expanding its offering' and they now wanted to tell their customers they could take care of the whole event – entertainments, decorations, props.

'Not weddings or anything,' she clarified. 'Not huge corporate events. That's not our area of the market. It's for people who want to have a family celebration, or something for their friends, and want someone else to take care of it all. So that's where you come in. That's what we want you to take care of.'

I frowned. 'I don't quite follow . . . where do I come in? What would I be doing?'

'All the stuff we don't want to do,' Molly said.

'What she means,' Kendall said, giving Molly a disapproving look, 'is the extras. While we concentrate on the food. But obviously we'll have to work together to ensure a seamless service. And for your work, we'd pay you. Obviously.'

I was starting to feel overwhelmed with all this business talk. I had looked after a few pre-schoolers for an afternoon, I wasn't a professional entertainer.

'To be honest,' I said, 'I'm not totally sure what you mean.'

Kendall sighed and leant back in her chair.

'I'll level with you, Grace. Things aren't going as well as we'd like with just the food. It's the expenses, you see. The costs are too high to make any real profit. I mean, sure, we can get someone to pay fifty pounds for a cake, but by the time we've bought all the ingredients, there's not much left over. We want to get in on the entertainments side. Because then, well, you don't have to buy anything, do you? People pay for us. To entertain them.'

Just then, Molly's phone began to ring. 'Ugh. Mother,' she said with a sigh, then climbed off the bed and skulked out to the hall to take the call.

Kendall was looking at me, straight in the eyes, with her hands in her pockets. I wasn't used to having someone – especially someone like her – give me so much attention. It was a bit overwhelming. I decided the best thing to do was to be honest about my concerns.

'I do think it all sounds great,' I said carefully. 'Like a great business and a great idea to do entertainments and I really would like to be involved. It's just . . . I don't know if I can? If I'd know what to do? Or why you would even ask me at all?'

Kendall sighed and sat down in her chair. She seemed different now Molly was no longer in the room. Less like she was putting on a show.

'I really need this to work, Grace,' she said, 'for loads of reasons. But one of them is because I have to show Eddie I can do it without him.'

'Your ex?'

She nodded. 'He promised me all summer that him moving away wouldn't change anything. We were going to make it work. But then, four days after he got to university, he called the whole thing off. Said he needed some distance. And when I said, "What about Bashed?", he said, "Let's just leave that now, it's not going to work anyway," and what he meant was, "It's not going to work now I'm not around to boss you about," and I want to show that it *will*. That I will make it work. Without him.'

I blinked. 'Oh. OK.' Everything was getting very complicated. I felt like I'd turned on the TV in the middle of a programme I had never heard of before.

Kendall leant forward and looked me straight in the eyes again. 'And we need you to make it work, Gracie. Look at me! I'm not an entertainer! No one finds me funny.'

'I'm sure they –'

'They find me interesting and impressive and cool, sure! But not entertaining! You, though, I've seen you around. You're zany and kooky and you wear clothes with . . .' She pointed at my T-shirt. '. . . random ladies in hats on the front.'

'It's the cover of *Mrs Dalloway* by Virginia Woolf.'

'Exactly!' she said. 'I don't even know any wolves! Please give us a chance? The people will one hundred per cent love you!'

I'd never been called zany or kooky before. And I'd definitely never been told that people will one hundred per cent love me before.

What could I say?

The Old-Lady Market

'OK,' I said, smiling. 'Why not? Let's do it.'

Kendall paused for a moment like she wasn't quite sure how to react to this news, then she said 'Brilliant!' and pulled me into a hug. I was so surprised I just stood there rigid with my arms dangling by my sides like tent poles.

Molly came back into the room. 'She's in,' Kendall told her.

'Sweet,' Molly replied, getting back into position on the bed.

'OK,' Kendall said, sitting back down at her desk. 'Let's get down to business. We've already got a client interested in a full party package and we need to get back to him with what we can do. We need to brainstorm. So let me tell you the brief.' She hit a few keys on her laptop and brought up an email. 'The client is a man named Philip Roach. He originally contacted us looking for a birthday cake for his old mum – she's going to be how old, Molly? Eighty? Ninety?'

'Sixty,' Molly said.

'Exactly,' Kendall said. 'So we're talking the old-lady market here. This is a great place to start because they're always . . . you know, grateful. Anyway, we'd already agreed the cake – we'll work out a design with roses or daisies or something, old ladies love all that – but when he said she was having all her mates over for a little party I saw an opportunity. I said, "Let us take care of the whole thing, make your mum feel special," and he jumped at the chance. So now we just need to decide what we're going to do.'

Kendall picked up her pencil and notepad and looked at me expectantly.

'Oh,' I said. 'OK. Yes. Let's . . . decide what we're going to do.'

'Yeah,' Kendall said. 'Let's decide.'

There was a pause for a moment and I wondered if Kendall and I were going to sit there taking it in turns to say 'let's decide' all evening but then she said, 'We know how great you are at entertaining kids. So this isn't that different. What are your ideas for looking after the old ones?'

'Right,' I said, 'OK, well. Let's think.' I was desperately searching my brain for inspiration. Right at that moment, I couldn't even think of any old people I knew, let alone what they might like. Eventually I said, 'Well, when my nan was alive, she mostly liked to talk about memories and stuff that had happened in the past . . .'

'Yes!' Kendall said. 'Old stuff! Like the war! You're totally right.' She wrote 'the war' down in her notes.

'And,' I went on, 'she liked to tell me how different things were when she was young, like how they had to write letters and wait for them to be delivered because they didn't have texts and stuff.'

Kendall nodded thoughtfully. 'Old-fashioned stationery,' she said slowly, as she added the words to her notes.

By the time we'd finished brainstorming what my nan had liked and what Kendall's old next-door neighbour liked and what Molly had seen some old people talking about on a documentary about a doctor's surgery she saw once, we'd decided that what sixty-year-olds were most interested in were:

The war
Old-fashioned stationery
Bingo
Knitting
Seeing girls in traditional girls' clothes i.e., dresses
Talking about aches and pains

Kendall tore the page out of her notes and passed it to me.

'Great!' she said, pushing the notebook into a drawer. 'I think we've come up with some really exciting ideas there. Do you think you'll be able to work with that?'

'Oh. I . . .' I blinked and looked down at the notes. 'What should I . . . ? You mean, you just want me to make it up from here . . . ?'

She smiled encouragingly. 'Absolutely! We want you to have total creative control over this side of the business. So meet us back here on Thursday at 4.30 and we'll head over to old lady Roach's house together, OK?'

'Oh!' I said again, then, 'OK!' Because I didn't honestly know what else I could say.

'Argh, so exciting!' Kendall said, suddenly getting to her feet and pulling me into another hug. This time she enveloped Molly into it too and the three of us stood there for a minute in an awkward little bundle until Kendall let us go.

As she showed me out, she said, 'Thanks so much for coming over, Gracie. Honestly, I'm so pleased you did. I've seen you around college and I thought, "that girl is cool," you know? I thought, "that girl knows her own mind and doesn't care what anyone else thinks". I like that. I like that a lot.'

'Really?' I said. I had no idea that the whole time when I thought Kendall didn't even know who I was, there she was creating entire impressions of me.

It was almost, I realised, as if she had been as in awe of me as I was of her.

The Wrong Questions

As I waited for the bus home, I could hardly believe how much things had changed in the space of forty-eight hours. It was remarkable, really, I thought to myself, how my popularity score had rocketed, just like that, from a totally random series of events. OK, so Molly and Kendall were only two people in terms of numbers, but in terms of developments . . . going inside Kendall Cross's actual bedroom for an actual hug, Kendall Cross telling me she thought I was cool. It was huge.

When I got home that night, I messaged Til.

I wanted to tell her about how I had a new job as an entertainer and how I'd been to Kendall's house and how Kendall had always known I was cool and knew my own mind, but I didn't know how to bring any of that up without Til making fun of me so instead I said:

Me: How's Lady Gaga?

Til: Ugh

Me: Not good?

Til: She's OK. I think she means to be good. She's just big. She found a pair of socks on her walk and ate them. Not just one, the pair. And they were really massive ones. Long and stripy. And then she puked them back up on the kitchen floor.

Me: On the plus side you've got a free pair of socks. Maybe see what else she can eat next time. A cool watch. Diamonds.

Til: Yeah funny

Me: I know I am

Til: How was Paddy's party?

Me: Full on. Kids are crazy.

Til: Yep

Me: Molly Shaw came

Til: To Paddy's party?

Me: To pick up her niece and nephew

Til: Oh right. So?

Me: Nothing really. I've just got back from Kendall's.

I knew that was a bit of a random thing to throw into the conversation, but I really wanted to write it down.

Til: Kendall Cross?

Me: Yeah. They want me to help with their business.

Til: What business?

Me: Parties

Til: Fair enough

It was so typical of Til not to ask me the question I wanted her to ask me.

Me: First one on Thursday

Til: You must be well pleased, you've always fancied her

Me: What? No I haven't

Til: You obviously have. Like looking at her the whole time and when she walks past you watch her like you're a little dog and you want her to take you for a walk

Me: WHAT? Shut up seriously. Just because I like some girls doesn't mean I like all girls and you are actually being homophobic right now

113

Til: I didn't say you like all girls I said you like Kendall Cross and you have done since the very first day of college when she walked in the back of the hall and you followed her with your eyes right from the door all the way to her seat in the corner and the whole time your mouth was basically open

I remembered exactly when she meant and she was right that I had noticed Kendall but I was almost one hundred per cent sure my mouth hadn't been open and if it was it was because I had a cold that week and was having trouble breathing through my nose.

I'd had enough of Til so I turned the screen off my phone and pushed it firmly under my pillow.

Why did she always have to say the wrong thing? Why couldn't she just ask me polite questions about my new job like a nice, normal, proper friend? Why did she have to think of the thing that would most annoy me and then just go ahead and say it?

I had noticed Kendall, it was true. She was very noticeable.

And she *was* an attractive person to look at, anyone with eyes could see that.

And the way she walked and talked did seem very grown up, which made her even more noticeable.

And yes, so maybe I did want her to like me. There was nothing so strange about that.

And yes, maybe when she'd looked me right in the eyes and told me I was cool and that people would love me, it *did* make my stomach feel like I'd just hit the downhill bit on a rollercoaster.

So yes, OK, so perhaps I did like her a bit more than I liked most people, and maybe in a way that wasn't strictly just as friends, but really, none of that was the point.

The point was, it was for me to tell Til and not the other way round.

My phone buzzed under the pillow.

Til: Stop sulking

Me: I'm not

Til: Hey have you heard about the Sack for Mac?

Me: No? They're sacking him?? He just lost all his stuff in a fire and now they're sacking him?? That is so harsh!

Til: No. The Sack for Mac is like an actual literal sack. A bag. It's a collection thing. Basically, if you've got any stuff you don't need any more that might be useful for Mac now he hasn't got any stuff, then you just bring it into college and they've put a massive bag in reception for you to put it in

Me: OK. I'll see what I've got.

Til: Night then

Me: Night

115

My Debut Assignment

The following Thursday, the day of Old Mrs Roach's party, I had last period free, which was lucky because it meant I could go home early to finalise my preparations. I knew that my performance at this, my debut assignment, could determine whether I had a future with Bashed or if Kendall would decide it had all been a big mistake and they would carry on without me thank you very much.

Given that I'd only had four days to get everything ready and that all I'd had in the way of instructions was the scrap of paper Kendall had handed me at the end of our meeting on Sunday evening, I was pleased with what I had managed to pull together.

With my bag full of ping-pong balls, thirty printed grids of numbers, a bag of feathers, a set of knitting needles, a ball of green wool and ten pots of Paddy's paints, I set out to meet the others, as instructed at Kendall's house.

'Wow, interesting dress,' Kendall said when she opened the door, taking the red fabric of one of the sleeves between her thumb and finger.

'Well, we wrote on the list, didn't we – "seeing girls in traditional clothes that girls wear, i.e., dresses".'

I had resisted this particular entry on the list all week, telling myself that it really didn't matter what I was wearing and that my normal jeans would be fine, but then at the last moment, I realised that Mrs Roach's son was paying real money for our services and that meant going to a proper effort to give her what would make her happy. So I'd headed to the drama department at lunchtime and pulled out a dress that had last been used in a production of *Annie*. When I put it on at home I knew that a little red dress with a neat white collar and a white bow around the middle was not something I would ever choose to wear myself, but it was certainly traditional and if this was what Mrs Roach wanted to see, then so be it.

Kendall looked up to the ceiling for a moment as if searching her memory. Then she shrugged and smiled and said, 'Oh yeah. I guess we did.'

'What are you going to wear?'

At that moment, Kendall was wearing leggings and slippers and an enormous jumper with 'Juicy' written on the front. I wasn't sure that the old ladies would consider that very traditional.

She looked down at her clothes, then back at me with a slight frown, like she didn't quite understand the question. Then her face cleared as she realised what I meant. 'Oh, we're not going to come, babe. Sorry, I should've said.'

I felt a flash of panic. 'What? What do you mean? Isn't the party on any more?

'Oh, yeah, it is. But Mol and I were talking and we really need to maximise efficiency, so that means all of us sticking to our own areas. And really, we're back of house. Front of house is totally your gig.'

'I don't quite follow? In front of what house?'

Kendall laughed. 'Back of house means like, behind the scenes, you know? Front of house is out there,' she gestured towards the window, 'out with the people. The face of the operation. That's your role.'

'So I just do it . . . on my own?'

Kendall's face broke into a wide smile and she grabbed me by the top of both my arms, making me jump. 'Yeah! You're going to be so great. I know you are. This is exactly why we picked you, because we knew you could handle the pressure.'

'OK,' I said. 'I see. OK.' I breathed out hard, then I swallowed and nodded firmly.

There was, I told myself, no reason why I couldn't do this. I was prepared, I had my props, I had a plan. I'd never been quite sure exactly what part Kendall and Molly were going to play anyway, so I had been ready to do it all if I needed to. And really, it was an honour, wasn't it? Kendall and Molly had a proper business going on here. One with real customers that took actual money. They wouldn't be trusting me with it if they didn't know I was absolutely up to the job.

'Of course, that's fine. Totally fine. I just didn't realise. But it's totally fine.'

'Great!' Kendall beamed again. 'So all the food's in here.'

I followed her into the kitchen, where Molly was adding the finishing touches to a white cake decorated with pink icing flowers and looping letters reading 'Happy Birthday Pamela'.

'It's a bit . . . different to the ones on the website,' I said. 'Less . . . big.'

Kendall waved her hand. 'Oh, babe, we didn't make any of those. Molly nicked the pictures from Pinterest. This should be fine though. Who really wants a cake shaped like a burger anyway?'

On the worktop next to her there were three large plastic boxes in a pile.

'OK,' Kendall said. 'So, Molly's just finishing the cake, then she'll box it up for you. And in here –' she put her hand on the pile of plastic boxes – 'we've got egg mayonnaise sandwiches without the egg –'

'Without the egg?' I repeated.

'Yes, exactly,' Kendall said. 'Remember what we decided about making things like the war because old people live in the past? They didn't have eggs in the war.'

'Oh yes. Of course.'

'And in the other boxes,' Kendall went on, 'are corned beef fritters – corned beef was another big deal in the olden days – and mini apple pies. Only with carrots instead of apples because they basically used carrots instead of everything in the past. I saw it in a museum once.'

I nodded. 'OK. Great! Just one question: how do I get all this to Mrs Roach's house?'

'Oh, we'll load it into the trailer,' Molly said.

'The trailer?'

She nodded once and pointed to the kitchen window. I went over and looked out into the garden and I could see a dark green bicycle with a small basket on the front and on the back, a rectangular metal box on wheels.

'Oh!' I said, surprised. 'So I ride that, with the . . . on the back . . . ? Only thing is, I'm not that great on a bike. And I've never pulled a trailer along behind me at all. I'm not sure I –'

Kendall laughed suddenly, and I smiled in relief, assuming she was going to say, 'I'm joking. Of course you don't have to ride a bike, silly. Get in the car, I'll drive you.' But what she actually did was come over to me, put her hand on my cheek like a nun with special healing powers and say, 'Gracie, don't stress it, babe. You'll be fine. Just relax. We know you can do this,' and once again, I felt the flipping-over feeling in my stomach.

And I decided that, one way or another, I *would* do this.

All the Rage

The twenty minutes it took me to cycle to Old Mrs Pamela Roach's house were hard going and by the time I eventually pulled up in the driveway of the address Kendall had typed into my phone, my cheeks were numb with the cold, my hair was plastered to my forehead and my traditional orphan Annie red dress was damp from the rain and sticking to my thighs.

I looked up at the house. It was so tall it seemed to disappear into the sky. The front was covered with thick ivy and, on the roof, there appeared to be an actual turret.

I knocked on the door and waited patiently, knowing it might take Old Mrs Roach and her friends a while to get to there – and that was if they even heard the sound at all.

When the door opened I was greeted by a tall, thin woman with bright red hair in a tidy little bob and cropped jeans. She was holding a big glass of red wine.

'Hello?' she said, smiling at me curiously.

'Oh, hello,' I said. I wondered if I'd got the wrong house. Or maybe Mrs Roach had a daughter as well as the son who'd booked our services. 'I'm here for the party? For Old Mrs – uh, for Mrs Roach? I've got a cake and –'

Her face broke into a smile. 'Oh yes! Of course, of course. Come in. I'm Pamela. Pamela Roach.'

Another woman came out of the lounge. This one had black hair and a smart trouser suit. She too was carrying wine.

'Look,' said Pamela, turning to Black Hair Woman. 'It's the girl Philip hired! Come in, my dear,' she said again to me and I stepped into the hallway, suddenly feeling very aware how dishevelled I must look next to these smart women.

The hallway had dark wooden floors and paintings in gold frames and reminded me of the big old houses that lords and ladies used to live in that you have to pay to go inside, where all the chairs and carpets are sealed off with rope to stop you touching them.

Pamela took the boxes from me and walked quickly down the hall. 'Of course, it's typical of Philip,' she said to Black Hair Woman as they went. 'When he said what did I want to do for my sixtieth, I said, "I want a little do. Nothing extravagant, just a few good friends, good wine and food," he said, "I'll sort that out, no problem." But I might have known it would mean hiring someone in! No chance of him actually doing something himself!'

I followed Pamela and Black Hair Woman down the hall, not sure what else to do with myself. It was like some kind of enchanted castle, with odd objects everywhere – a sewing machine hanging from the ceiling. A harp on a table in the corner. I had to try hard not to gaze around at it all in wonder.

'Well, it's still kind of him, I suppose,' Black Hair Woman said. 'I'm lucky to get a card from my lot. What's your name, darling?' she said, turning to me.

'Grace,' I told her. 'And the business . . . I mean, the company I work for . . . they're called Bashed.'

'Bashed!' Black Hair Woman clapped her hands together. 'How clever! Because you do "bashes"? I love it! I'm Marie.'

'So, what have we got here?' Pamela said, peeling the lid from the cake box.

'Well, there's a cake in one,' I said. 'And then the others are egg mayonnaise sandwiches with no eggs, corned beef fritters and apple pies with carrots instead of apples.'

Pamela blinked once and then frowned just for a moment, as if she was processing all this. Then she gave her head a little shake as if to clear away her concerns and said, 'Righty-ho! Well, what an interesting meal it sounds!'

I suddenly felt that perhaps I should have explained the menu better, rather than simply listing the items. It's like Kendall said, I was meant to be front of house. Presenting things was my area.

'It's because in the war,' I said, 'and in the old days in general, they didn't have eggs or apples. Only carrots,' I told them. 'So we thought, we better not have any eggs or apples either.'

Pamela blinked again. 'Right, OK.'

I wasn't sure how else I could explain it. I didn't want to specifically say our idea about old people mostly liking things from the past because to do that, I would have to officially call her old. And now I was there, I was wondering if maybe sixty wasn't very old at all. In fact, I worked out that sixty years ago, it was the 1950s. Wasn't the war all done by then?

Luckily, Marie seemed to get on board with the idea.

'How sweet!' she said, picking up a corned beef fritter. 'A historical theme. Retro is all the rage these days, isn't it?'

'Absolutely,' I agreed. 'All the rage.'

'The rest of the guests will be arriving in the next fifteen minutes or thereabouts,' Pamela said to me. 'So if you could just sort of, greet people, hand out snacks and what have you. Then we'll start entertainment when everyone's assembled?'

'OK, sure.' I smiled confidently like I did this every day of the week, but I suddenly wasn't sure if these ladies seemed the right type for what I had lined up at all.

As we waited for the guests, I realised I should talk to Pamela and give a good impression of the company. I had planned for this part of the evening, and had a number of discussion topics lined up, but I wasn't sure about any of them now.

I went ahead with the first one regardless.

'How are your aches and pains?' I said, setting my face into a sympathetic expression.

Pamela looked at me curiously. 'What aches and pains?'

I paused for a moment. I hadn't anticipated that question. Surely she had some? And surely the idea was that she told *me* all about them, not the other way around?

I decided to change tack, to go off script.

'This is a lovely house,' I said.

'Oh yes. Thank you. Thank you.' She said it with a sigh, like she was weary about it for some reason. 'It's become something of a burden lately, though, I must say. It was lovely when the kids were small. Plenty of space for them to run around. Lots of hiding places. It was full of life. But now the kids are adults, with their own kids, and all living miles away. And my husband ran off with a traffic warden years ago so here I am, rattling around on my own. It's too much to manage, really. Something's always broken.'

And as if to illustrate the point, a hook that had been holding a saucepan from the ceiling came loose and the saucepan fell to the floor with a clatter. I bent down to help her retrieve it but just then the doorbell rang, signalling the arrival of the first of the guests.

'Would you get that?' Pamela said.

I picked up the large plate of sandwiches. I was on.

Call Me Clive

Half an hour later, when the whole downstairs of Pamela's house was filled with ladies and men in casual but elegant clothes, and everyone had tried an eggless egg sandwich or a carrot-but-no-apple pie, Pamela crossed the room and said, 'So really, whenever you're ready . . . ?' and I realised it was time for me to take to the stage.

As I moved to the end of the long living room where a space had been cleared for me, I considered how different the scene before me was to the one I'd imagined. I'd thought I'd be facing a room of grey-haired old ladies with blankets on their knees, slumping in their chairs as they nodded off. Instead, these people looked like they'd come straight from important business meetings or charity lunches. But it was too late to change my plans now.

I took my bag of ping-pong balls and my envelope of printed cards and stood at the front.

'Ladies and gentlemen, thank you all for coming this evening to Pamela's celebration. I'd like to invite you all to join in a game of,' I pulled the cards out of the envelope and held them out above my head, 'Big Bashed Bingo!'

When we'd been planning what I could do to entertain Pamela's guests earlier that week, we'd decided that bingo was something all old people liked. I remembered Reeta telling me once that her great-gran, who was 'about 150', had played bingo in her care home, so I thought it was something everyone would be able to keep up with. Now, though, I realised that keeping up wasn't going to be a problem; rather, I had a new concern: were they going to be bored? Would sophisticated people like this be expecting a show of breathtaking illusions or a one-man band?

There was a brief moment of silence where I thought they were going to ask me to leave, or worse, ask me if I had any better ideas, and I began to consider what exactly I would perform if they asked me to sing instead, but then Pamela held her wine glass in the air and said, 'How tremendous! Do you know I've never had a game of bingo in my life! What an adventure!'

I beamed at her out of sheer relief. I wasn't sure if Pamela was really as pleased as she was making out or if she was just being polite, but I didn't much care. I just had to get through the next hour.

'I do love a competition,' a man said, coming forward to take the bingo grids I'd stayed up half the night on Tuesday designing, printing and sticking on silver card. He began to hand them out to the other guests. 'Is there a prize?'

'Uh, yes!' I said. 'Yep, there's a prize.' I didn't mention that I was now wondering if that too might have been a mistake.

Before we could begin, there was one more item from our list I had to bring out. I picked up my carrier bags of feathers. 'In terms of pens, I thought why use normal, boring pens? So I've bought you these,' I began to hand them around.

'Feathers?' Marie asked, turning hers over in her hands curiously.

'Quills!' I cried. 'And here is your ink.' I took Paddy's paints out of my bag and placed them around the room so everyone had easy access to one. 'Just dip your quill in the pots, and away you go.'

'Oh goodness,' Marie said, with a giggle. 'How remarkable.'

I could see now the whole spectacle probably seemed quite random but I decided it was better not to complicate things by explaining Kendall's theory about old people enjoying old-fashioned stationery.

When everyone was in position, bingo cards and quills in hand, I began to pull the ping-pong balls – each showing a number carefully written in permanent marker – out of the bag.

It was only as I looked at the first one that I remembered that a key part of bingo calling was giving the number a sort of nickname, rather than just reading it out as it was written. There were official names to use, I knew, but I had no idea what they were. Two fat ladies, was one, wasn't it? But which number was that? And I didn't want any of the women present to think I was calling them a fat lady.

I realised it didn't matter. These people didn't seem to know much about bingo at all, so I guessed they wouldn't know any more about the nicknames than I did. I could just make them up.

'First up we have . . . twenty-eight – was it something you ate!'

Everyone's heads bowed as they went to check their cards. Someone at the end of the room called, 'Yes! I've got that one.' She darted forward to dip her feather in the paint and carefully marked it off.

I found that when I got going, I was quite good at making up nicknames on the spot. And what's more, the partygoers seemed to enjoy it, laughing out loud with every new number.

'Forty-five, call me Clive!'

'Thirty-three, I need a wee!'

'Forty-two, smell my shoe!'

With all the laughing and noise, and the time it took for people to pass round the ink pots every time they wanted to mark off a number, it was nearly twenty minutes before a woman in a green dress shouted, 'Oh! I've got them! All the numbers! Is that it? Is that bingo? Bingo! Me, bingo!'

I went to collect her card, compared it against my discarded bag of balls and confirmed her win.

'What's my prize?' she asked, looking at me excitedly.

'Well, it's a quite a good one, if I do say so myself,' I said, going over to my bag to fetch it. The truth was, I wasn't sure it was good at all, but I hoped by telling her it was she would be too polite to argue.

Luckily it seemed to work, and when I handed over the knitting needles and ball of wool, together with a slim book called *Knitting Patterns for Everyday Outfits*, she beamed and began to turn the wool over in her hands like it was a magical item.

'Oh, how lovely!' she said, staring at it in wonder. 'I've always meant to learn how to knit. It's terribly fashionable these days, isn't it? I see a young girl doing it on the train every morning. Perhaps I'll ask her for some tips!'

'You've been wonderful,' Pamela said, when the bingo was over and the food had been eaten, and although I thought the party would go on for some hours yet, it seemed time for me to leave. 'Honestly, it's been so fascinating to have been introduced to all these fashionable retro things you young folk are into these days!'

She put her hands on my shoulders and kissed me on both cheeks. 'And do come and visit me again!' she said. 'Come and tell me how you're getting on with college.'

I promised Pamela that I would, loaded my empty trays into the bike trailer, and rode off into the night.

Sack for Mac

The next day, when I walked through the main college doors, Til, Reeta and I walked almost straight into a giant blue plastic sack, half filled with random objects.

'Oh yeah,' Til said, looking down at it. 'I guess this is the Sack for Mac.'

With Pamela Roach's party taking over my week, I'd totally forgotten to bring anything in to add to the collection. The three of us leant in and looked at what he'd been given so far. It was quite a jumble of items – an old pair of slippers. A toasted sandwich maker that had been repaired with parcel tape. A travel version of Scrabble.

I picked up an old radio and as I did so a broken plastic panel fell off the back of it, spilling batteries onto the floor.

'Why have people brought all this in?' I said, trying to round up the batteries and fit the cracked plastic panel back into position. 'I know Mac's lost all his stuff but that doesn't mean he's suddenly become some kind of crazy hoarder who wants to collect any old junk to fill his new house with.'

Til picked up a cushion with an embroidered penguin on the front and a large red stain on the back. She crinkled her nose and tossed it back into the bag. 'I know. Some of this stuff is rough. I don't know why they asked people to bring things in. That's never going to work. He needs money, so he can buy his own stuff. Stuff he actually *needs*. Not other people's rubbish.'

Reeta shrugged, turning a snow globe over in her hands thoughtfully. 'I suppose people haven't got spare money lying around their houses though,' she said. 'That's the problem.'

I sighed. 'Yeah. I guess.'

I was busy at college that day with all five periods filled with classes, but every chance I could, I ducked into the canteen to see if Kendall and Molly were in the Booth so I could report back to them that Pamela Roach's party had been a success. I didn't see them all day, but halfway through the afternoon, I got a message from Kendall:

> Gracie, you NAILED Old Mrs Roach's party.
> She loves you and us.
> Come to mine after college.
> We need to talk business.

It was all I could do not to turn around and walk directly out of college, but I had one more lesson to go to and, anyway, I decided it was time for me to play things a little cooler. The first time Kendall had summoned me to her house, when she'd invited me to join Bashed, I couldn't believe my luck. Now though, I'd actually achieved something. Customers were pleased with me.

I had something to offer.

My Angle

As soon as Kendall opened her front door to me, she pulled me into a tight hug. 'You. Little. Legend,' she said, giving me an extra squeeze with each word. 'You are such a pro!'

'She was happy then?' I said shyly. 'Pamela? Mrs Roach? With it all?'

'Oh, babe, she was all over it,' Kendall said, leading the way up the stairs to her room. 'She sent me this email going on about how it was quirky and weird but that she loved how "inventive" it was. I said to Mol, I said, "that's Grace all right – weird!"'

'Yeah!' I said, laughing. She seemed to be saying it as a compliment, so I thought it was only polite to receive it as such.

'You should put it on the website as a quote,' Molly said as Kendall and I went into the room. 'Then if Eddie looks he'll see how well you're doing without him.'

'Oh. Well, yeah. I mean, I already told him actually. He rang, so . . .' She was busy searching through a drawer for something but I got the impression she was only doing it to avoid looking at Molly.

'Kendall!' Molly said, 'You're not supposed to answer when he calls! We made a plan for this. You're forgetting him, remember? He's forgotten.'

Kendall sighed. 'I know, I know.'

Molly turned to me then. 'Eddie is basically moving on with his life with a million new girlfriends and university and everything, but not letting Kendall move on with hers and ringing her the whole time to say he misses her. But not enough to, you know, actually get back with her.'

Kendall was quiet for a moment. Then she said, 'He hasn't got a new girlfriend, actually. They're just girls. Not girl*friends*.'

Molly didn't reply but I thought I saw the tiniest hint of an eye roll.

'Anyway,' Kendall said, her voice bright again, 'the great news is, we've got a new booking out of it! This woman – Marie? – she wants us to do her Christmas party. She wants a full-on Santa service – big beard, sack of presents, the whole shebang. I said it was right up your street. *And* she's going to give us a load of money upfront to get all the gifts, so we just have to buy them, wrap them and hand them out! It's a pretty sweet gig, Gracie.'

'Yeah!' I agreed. 'Sweet gig!'

'Oh, and I nearly forgot.' Kendall reached into a drawer in her dressing table and took out a five-pound note. 'It's pay day!'

She pushed it into my hand and I looked down at it. I had never given much thought to the money side of the business at all – I was too focused on being pleased that only a few weeks after I'd decided to be popular I was now a regular guest to Kendall Cross's house – but now I couldn't help but wonder: how had this five-pound figure been decided? I knew Pamela had paid £150 for our services. Was five pounds really all my work amounted to?

Kendall obviously sensed my confusion. 'This is a business, Gracie. We've got overheads.'

I looked at her blankly.

'Expenses,' she said. 'We'll talk you through the finances one day. But long story short, if we make profit, we put it back into the business. We reinvest. Because that's how you grow. You know?'

'Yes,' I said, nodding. 'Yes, of course.' Because really, who was I to come in and question how she ran her business? She seemed to be doing well at it, after all.

It was then that I caught a glimpse of the inside of the drawer my five pounds had come from. There, sitting on top of a pink notebook, was a wodge of notes – tens and twenties, it looked like – held together with an elastic band. I supposed this was the money they had taken in fees that they used to pay for the ingredients and supplies for the next cakes and parties.

But something about the sight of it just sitting there reminded me of what Reeta had said earlier, when we'd been staring sadly at Mac's sack in reception:

'People don't just have money lying about their house.'

Except, here, in Kendall's house, it appeared they did.

I began saying the idea almost as soon as it popped into my head.

'We should give some money to Mac.'

'What's that, babe?' Kendall said, busy typing something into a spreadsheet on her computer.

I already wasn't sure it was a good idea, but I'd said it now. 'You know – Mac? The caretaker at college?'

Kendall looked up from her computer and frowned thoughtfully. 'Oh yeah, I know. Didn't he burn his whole house down?'

'Well, not on purpose. I don't think *he* burnt it down, technically.'

'But they're already doing a collection for him, aren't they?' Kendall said. 'That big bag of rubbish in reception? Actually, I've got some stuff I can give. That old foot spa, for one thing.' She nodded to a box on top of her wardrobe. 'It's a good idea, isn't it? Give people the chance to get rid of some junk at the same time as sorting old Mac out with what he needs.'

'Well, that's sort of the point,' I said. 'He's just getting junk. He's not going to get anything he actually needs that way. He needs furniture and proper clothes and a duvet and stuff.'

'Beggars can't be choosers,' Molly said with a shrug.

I ignored her and carried on. 'I think what he needs, what would really help him out, is if he had some money. To buy new stuff that he's actually chosen himself. So I was thinking, we could give him some, couldn't we? Just a bit? Companies do donations sometimes, don't they?'

The idea was growing on me now. It made perfect sense.

Molly made a face. 'Maybe if you're a big company like Tesco or McDonalds and have loads going spare in all your big bank accounts. We can't just give all *our* money away. We need it to buy ingredients and everything.'

'Well, I didn't mean *all* of it,' I said. 'I don't know. Maybe some of the profits or something . . .'

'I don't think –' Molly began, but Kendall cut her off.

'Oh my god, Gracie.' She grabbed me by the top of my arms. She grabbed my arms a lot, I noticed.

''What?' I said.

'That is the best idea!' She was looking at me, eyes shining suddenly. 'You are a *genius*, babe.'

It was always so instant, the rush of warmth to my cheeks when I had pleased her. She was just so enthusiastic with her praise. She made me feel, just for that moment, like I was the most important person in the world. I imagined it must be what it was like to be a dog, delighting your owner by bringing the ball back first time. I wouldn't have put it past Kendall to scratch me behind the ears.

'Is it?' I said.

But she didn't reply because already she had sprung into action, pulling her notebook out of the drawer and scribbling down some notes. 'What we should do,' she said, 'is say that for a certain period – say now until Christmas – all the profits go to Mac. We can advertise it, really big it up as an idea, so people will know that by choosing Bashed for their event, not only are they getting a super-cool premium service, but they're helping out a poor man who's lost his home and family in a terrible fire.'

'Well, no actual people died –'

Kendall waved her hand. 'Well, whatever. People will

know we're doing a good thing. And they'll think *they're* doing a good thing by using our business. And, Gracie, people like nothing more than to feel like they're doing a good thing, believe me.'

'So, you'll really do it? All the profits, all the way until Christmas, Mac can have them?' It was more generous than I could have hoped for.

'Yeah! Absolutely! I'll update the website now so everyone knows about it.'

Kendall flipped open her laptop and began typing quickly. Molly lay back on the bed in her favourite position, looking at her phone. I got the feeling she was sulking because I was the one who'd had the good idea.

Suddenly Kendall stopped typing and spun around on her chair to fix me with one of her intense looks. 'You know what, Gracie, *this* is why we needed you on board.'

'How do you mean?'

'This is what you bring to the business. This is your angle. Kindness. Niceness. You're just so *nice*. I've always thought that about you.'

'Really?' She's already told me she thought I was cool and one-of-a-kind. Now she'd been thinking I was nice too. I was starting to wonder exactly how much time Kendall had spent thinking about me when I thought she didn't even know my name.

She nodded enthusiastically. 'You've injected our company with niceness, right at its core. And that's so brilliant.' She turned back to her computer and continued typing. 'Because nothing sells as well as niceness.'

Personal Brand

The following Saturday I hadn't made any plans because I half thought Kendall might want me for a business meeting, or even that she might suggest we hung out in a more social way. That was the step I was really hoping for – when we were able to make the leap from business colleagues to friends. She seemed to like me so much, I thought surely it was only a matter of time before she asked me to go over and watch a film or to go into town with her. But I knew from bitter experience you couldn't force these things, so when no invitation came, I realised it looked like I was at a loose end.

I messaged Til.

Me: What are you doing, do you wanna come over?

Til: Can't. Packing.

Me: Packing for what? Are you going on holiday?

Til: Ha. As if. No. Moving.

Me: Oh OK. Moving house? Where to?

Til: If you're going to ask questions you can come round and help me pack while you ask them

Helping Til load all her things into cardboard boxes while the enormous energetic Lady Gaga was trying to push her nose into my ear or lick my forehead with her flappy pink tongue wasn't the best way I could think of spending my Saturday, but it sounded like Til could use an extra pair of hands. And I was curious to hear her latest housing news.

When I arrived, I found Til in the middle of her lounge, surrounded by half-packed boxes, her hair sticking straight up, which it always does when she's stressed and has been running her hand through it over and over.

'So, what's going on?' I asked, picking up a book and placing it in the top of the box nearest me. Til immediately took the book out and put it in a different box.

'We found this place. Some guy Mum works with has a couple of spare rooms. He says he's OK with Lady Gaga, so we're going to go there.'

'Will that be OK? Living with some random bloke? What's he like?'

Til shrugged. 'Never met him. Mum says he's OK. And it's not like we've got any better options. Landlords don't exactly want a massive furry Lady Gaga messing up their carpets.'

I wasn't sure I would like the idea of moving in with a man I'd never met but I didn't think it was a good time to say this, not when it didn't sound like Til had much choice in the matter. Instead, I decided to change the subject to at least take her mind off things while we packed.

'Til, would you say I was a nice person?'

'No,' she said immediately.

I frowned. 'Why? Why not?'

'Well, I wouldn't say you were *not* nice, but it wouldn't be the first word I'd think of if someone said, "What's that Grace like?" I wouldn't think to say, "Oh, she's really nice."'

'What would you say?'

Til thought about this for a moment. 'Annoying. Or uptight. Or what's the word for like, really in your face? Like never shutting up and –'

'OK, great, thanks.' I held up my hand to cut her off. 'But anyway, the reason I ask is because Kendall said I was nice.'

'Oh, *Kendall* said it, did she,' Til said, with an annoying smirk. 'It must be true then.'

'I do think it's worth considering, actually,' I said, not looking at her as I stacked CDs into a long narrow box. 'I've been thinking about it, and I think maybe she's onto something. Like, I think I *am* essentially nice, deep down. But the problem is, not enough people realise it. I don't advertise the fact. And that's why I'm not as popular as . . . as I'd like to be. In an ideal world.'

'Because people don't know you're nice? You're a closet nice person?'

'Yes,' I said. 'Exactly. So I've been thinking, and what I'm

141

going to do is make much more effort to project my niceness. To let people know it's there. To fashion my personal brand with niceness far more front and centre.'

Til sighed and reached for some tape to seal up her box. 'Fair enough. Go and put the kettle on then, will you, little miss nice? Might as well start how you mean to go on.'

A Trial

The next day, when I arrived for my shift at Podrick's, Sheila Wheeler was already busy at the back of the shop, unloading some lunchboxes shaped like radios onto a shelf. I was about to take my seat behind the counter without going over to say hello as I usually did, when I thought: who better to practise my new nice persona on than Sheila, someone who never seemed remotely interested in whether people were nice or not, and in fact probably didn't know the difference? It was the perfect safe training ground.

I tucked my bag underneath the desk and made my way to the back of the shop.

'Hi, Sheila,' I said.

'Morning,' she said gruffly, without looking up from her task.

'Can I do that for you?' I said. 'You can have a rest if you like?'

This had seemed the obvious way to display my niceness. Sheila was busy doing something; I could offer to help with it. Unfortunately, what I hadn't stopped to think about was the type of person I was making that offer to.

She turned to look at me with a frown. 'Rest? What would

I want a rest for? I only just got here.'

'Oh. I know, I just thought –'

'Believe it or not, my girl, I am perfectly capable of doing my job. I know you probably think I'm about a hundred years old but just because I haven't got eighty-four GCSE grades like you, I do know how to unload a box.'

My mistake was clear. What I'd done was try to be nice in a way that would appeal to any normal person. I hadn't stopped to remember that Sheila wasn't any normal person. Sheila was someone who prided herself on never needing help. And so, the tactic I'd tried – offering to help – had mortally offended her.

I was about to give up and retreat to my seat when I had an idea. What made someone like Sheila happy was not being offered help, but being asked for it.

'You know, I was actually wondering if you could help me,' I began. 'For reasons I can't go into, I need to make a Santa outfit. Not just the outfit, but the sack and boxes to put the presents in. All of the accessories. But I don't really know how to do it. Where to even start.'

'Father Christmas?' Sheila said, hauling herself to her feet. 'From scratch? You got nothing?'

'Nothing at all,' I said. 'Yet.'

Kendall had given me some money to get the presents and gifts organised for Marie's Christmas party where I would be taking the starring role of Father Christmas, but I hadn't yet had a chance to get to the shops. And I meant what I said: I wasn't really sure where to start. What was a Santa suit even made of?

'Well, then,' she said, heading over to the fabric aisle. 'First you'll need some red felt. A good six metres, I'd say. And some white fur for the trim. You got thread?'

Sheila began marching up and down the shop, gathering rolls of fabric and thread and scissors and fastenings and setting it all down on the counter.

'It's so amazing,' I said, looking down at it all, 'the way you just know everything about this shop. And the way you know how to do stuff! Like, just how much knowledge you have, really.'

'Oh.' Sheila seemed surprised, embarrassed even. 'Oh, right.' But there was the smallest hint of a smile. 'That's what happens when you've been around a few years. Can't help but pick up knowledge.'

'Maybe,' I said. 'But I could never remember everything in this shop. I can never remember anything.'

'Well,' she said. 'I have always been able to keep stuff –' she tapped the side of her head with her finger – 'up there. You know – good storage.'

'Amazing,' I said again, and Sheila ambled back off to her box of lunchbox radios, humming to herself.

I was on lock-up that day, which I hate because it means you have to wait for all the customers to get out – and some of them take ages – and then when they've finally gone you have to set all the alarms and lock all the doors and windows, and the whole thing means I get home at least forty minutes later than I would normally. But just before five, Sheila came over and said, 'You getting off then?'

'I'm locking up today.'

'Don't worry about that,' she said. 'I'll take care of it.'

'Oh,' I said, picking up my bag. 'Are you sure? It's my turn?'

'Yes, yes, it's fine. Go on. I'm sure you've got a fun evening planned, you youngsters always do. God help you.'

I didn't. I didn't have anything planned at all. But Sheila thinking I did and telling me to get off to it was about the nicest thing she'd ever said to me.

Was it really as easy as this? I start being nice to people and they start being nice right back? I could hardly believe I hadn't tried it out before.

Putting it Out There

I tried to think about how exactly I should launch my new personal brand. Sheila had just been a trial. Unveiling it to the real world was going to take more careful handling.

The easiest thing, I knew, would be to carry on going about my normal life, but just tweaking my interactions to up the niceness factor where I could. But that didn't seem radical enough somehow. How much impact was that going to have, realistically? Who would even benefit? I would see Mum and Dad, perhaps Ollie, at home, and then Til and Reeta at college, and I could be a bit friendlier with all of them. And I could do an extra-smiley 'morning!' to the bus driver and 'thanks!' to the chip lady in the canteen but would they even notice? I didn't see how it was going to change their lives and it certainly wasn't going to change mine.

What I needed was to be proactive, to put myself and my charm out there. I needed to launch a niceness offensive.

When I arrived at college, I was excited to get going with my experiment – because I knew that's what it was, in these early stages: experimental. There would be some trial and error while I fine-tuned my new strategy, but I was keen to get the first test underway.

As I made my way to my locker I was on high alert, taking in the people and actions around me, looking for opportunities to step in to offer a kind word or some assistance. Anything that might leave people thinking, 'Who was that? She was so nice!'

I was disappointed though when no obvious opportunity presented itself. There was no one struggling to carry a heavy load through a door. No one sitting in the corner crying who might have needed a pat on the arm and a word of encouragement. Everyone seemed to be going about their business quite happily. Annoying.

As I walked past the art area, through the big windows, I spotted Lily Birch, working on a big canvas. I stopped, looking at her for a moment. I realised she was a perfect target.

Lily Birch was popular. Lily Birch wasn't the type to sit in the Booth but she was truly – as in numbers-wise – popular. She knew a lot of people. Everyone, really. She was on committees and she did sports and her mum ran a nursery in town and half the kids in college had gone there or had a brother or sister who did. It was also something about her manner. She was talkative and friendly and enthusiastic. Whereas people like Kendall and Molly seemed aloof at college, sitting in their Booth castle like queens, Lily Birch was more like the chatty maid who knew everyone's business.

And all this was perfect for me because if my new personality was going to take off, I needed to make sure as many people as possible knew about it. I needed to think about influence. And Lily Birch had influence.

I did some rough calculations and worked out that in any given week, Lily might speak to, what? A hundred different people? So, if I was nice to someone like Lily, then news of my niceness would spread far more quickly than if I only unleashed it on, for example, Very Small Robbie, who sat in the corner of the library drawing comic strips all day and never spoke to anyone.

If, I reasoned, I was super nice to someone like Lily, then she would, surely, begin to mention it to other people. 'Oh, let's see if Grace wants to come, she's so nice' she might say when she received one of the many invitations I was sure she got each day. 'That Grace is really decent, actually', she could tell anyone and everyone. News of my niceness would spread. It would become my reputation.

And that, I believe, is what they call making a name for yourself.

At college the art classrooms were all surrounded by a kind of open-plan conservatory room with tables and screen-printing sets and sinks, as well as fridges that I think were meant for some kind of special paint but that most people used for cans of Pepsi and leftover pizzas. Lily was working in this area now, standing at a table in the corner. She was wearing an old painting shirt over her own clothes and had her hair in two long plaits down her back. I walked over to her table and hovered for a moment. She was painting very quickly, covering a canvas with yellow.

I wasn't sure how to kick things off but I knew there was only so long I could stand there silently before it started to look strange, so I said, 'Hey!'

She looked up, surprised, obviously so engrossed in her project that she hadn't noticed me approach. 'Oh, hi, Grace.'

She looked at me expectantly. I realised that as I'd approached her, I was the one who'd have to move the conversation on. I had planned to warm up a little before launching right into the niceness, but I couldn't think of anything else to say, so I got straight down to business.

'That's amazing!' I said, nodding at her canvas.

She looked at me again and blinked. 'Oh. Thanks?' Her smile was slightly bemused, but it was a smile at least. 'I couldn't buy a yellow canvas so I'm making my own. It's just the base at the moment. I haven't actually started.'

'Well, yeah, of course,' I said. 'But it's just so . . . yellow.'

I paused. What else could you say about a totally yellow painting? I took art myself and I found the drawing relaxing but I honestly didn't know how people wrote whole essays about paintings when all you could really write is what was sitting there right in front of you.

I searched my brain for something else to say. 'It reminds me of . . . a banana,' I said eventually. 'A lovely big yellow banana.'

Lily frowned slightly, but she looked at her painting with her head on one side like she was considering my comments.

'And a canary!' I added. 'And the sun and mustard and custard.'

I paused again. Were there any more yellow things I could list? There must have been, but none of them were coming to me, right at that moment. I decided I'd said enough. I needed to give her space to react to my compliment, to bask in the warm glow of my words.

I looked at her, waiting to see how she'd respond. In the end she just shrugged and said, 'OK. Thanks,' again, and carried on painting.

I hesitated, not sure where to go from here. Had I said enough to leave Lily with a lasting impression of how nice I was? Enough for her to mention it to other people? I wasn't sure I had so I nearly persevered. I nearly plucked another compliment from the air and threw it at her, but my resolve failed me. It wasn't working. I needed a plan. A script. Lily was clearly more confused than pleased and I didn't want her to start spreading around that I was a nutcase. That wasn't the reputation I was aiming for.

'Anyway, I've just come to see a friend,' I said. I nodded towards the table where, fortunately for me, Reeta had decided to sit at for her free first period.

'Ah. OK. Cool,' Lily said, clearly relieved to hear that I would shortly be on my way. She turned back to her painting and I made my exit.

I sat down opposite Reeta and rested my chin on my hands, frowning as I tried to analyse my performance.

'You didn't seem real,' Reeta said, suddenly.

'What?'

'When you were talking to Lily. I know you were trying to be nice. Til told me that's your thing now. And I could see you trying so hard but it was like you didn't really mean it, so it didn't count.'

'I did!' I protested. 'I did mean it! Her painting *is* yellow! It is like a big lovely banana!'

Reeta just looked at me and shook her head slowly.

I sighed. I realised that if I was serious about improving my social skills, I had to be prepared to take feedback onboard. 'You're right,' I said calmly. 'I need to think of something more specific to compliment people on. Something they'll really believe.'

'Well,' Reeta said slowly, searching through her pencil tin for a ruler. 'You don't have to just do compliments. Why don't you ask questions?'

I frowned. 'You mean, give them a quiz? On general knowledge or something particular? Should I give them the questions on a piece of paper to fill in or read them out loud?'

'No!' Reeta laughed. 'Just be *interested* in them. That's the nicest thing sometimes, don't you think?'

Questions

I spent most of first period considering what Reeta had said. The more I thought about it, the more it made sense.

Asking questions sent out a clear message, didn't it – it said, 'I want to know about you.' It said, 'I care what you think.' And really, what is more essential to being nice than caring?

In fact, it seemed so obvious now I'd had it pointed out to me that I threw myself into it as soon as I possibly could and, in conversations where I once would have listened politely or said nothing at all, I became like an investigative journalist.

In psychology after break, there were a few minutes at the beginning of the class when the room was empty except for me and Katie Boyd. I was still blushing any time I remembered the embarrassing way I'd bulldozed my way into her first date with Martin so my natural instinct was to say a polite hello, then to pretend I was preoccupied with my phone or a book so I didn't have to look at her, but I knew now was exactly the time to be overriding my natural instincts. So, when I went into the room and found her there, I greeted her enthusiastically and went to sit right next to her.

I could see she was surprised by this choice seeing as the classroom was totally empty and I could've chosen to sit anywhere, but I then surprised her even further by jumping straight in with a direct question – 'How's it going with you and Martin?'

But, surprised as she might have been, she answered, and she even seemed to relax a little as she told me how great he'd been when she'd introduced him to her parents and that he'd bought her a phone cover that he'd had especially printed with the artwork from her favourite album.

By the time the other members of the class arrived, I felt like not only had we put the misunderstanding about the *Jaws* night behind us, but that the next time I bumped into her, I would feel quite happy striking up a conversation about her relationship – about anything really – and it would seem totally natural and not at all random, because we'd had this great chat. We'd laid the groundwork.

It was amazing, in a way, I reflected as I left psychology an hour later. All it took was one leap of faith, forcing myself to ask one bold question, and whole barriers were broken down.

So I didn't stop there.

When I saw Martin later that afternoon, I was able to use the information earlier gathered from Katie and ask him a caring, tailored question of his own. 'So, how did it go meeting Katie's parents?'

There was a brief moment of surprise – I suppose while he wondered how I knew he'd spent the evening with them – but then we were off, and he seemed quite happy to tell me all sorts of things from how scared he'd been before he'd gone round to how they worked out over dinner that he and Katie had actually been in the same nursery class together when they were three.

Reeta was right, I realised. When I'd tried to shower Lily Birch with compliments, it had been weird. Unnatural. She clearly wasn't comfortable with the conversation and neither was I. But now, with these questions – these magic questions! – conversations were just galloping on and on as if these people were my best friends.

When I found myself standing next to Josh from the Booth as we unloaded our books into our lockers, although I didn't know him, beyond knowing his name, I reasoned that it was the perfect time to make conversation. That was the whole *point* of the questions – to use them to expand my circles.

So when he took a music case out of his locker and put it by his feet, I took my chance.

'What's in the case?'

He looked up, surprised. 'Oh . . . it's a flute.'

I nodded. 'How long have you played?'

He shook his head. 'I don't. It's my sister's. She left it at our dad's so I'm taking it back to Mum's for her.'

Something I'd worked out when talking to Katie earlier was that you really only needed the tiniest nugget of information to open up a whole world of questions and already lots were popping into my head. For example:

So your parents are divorced, are they? When did
    that happen?

Who do you live with? Where do you live? Do you
    like it?

Have you only got one sister or are there more of you?

But I decided that, as Josh's locker was next to mine, and therefore we found ourselves side by side at least once a day, there was plenty of time to cover it all. I didn't want to overwhelm him. For now, I settled on, 'How old is she?' and Josh told me she was thirteen and then he waved goodbye and went on his way.

It wasn't a memorable conversation, but I was happy with it. I had broken the ice. There would be more where that came from next time.

Over that first week in December, I kept up the strategy, and found that, actually, I had a genuine, natural curiosity about people that had obviously been sitting inside me, just waiting for an opportunity to come out.

I talked to everyone: students in my classes, the tutors who led them, people I found myself next to in the dinner queue, the man I found fixing the network cable in the computer room.

I can't lie – there were times when I couldn't think of a suitable question and so the one I had come out with hadn't been well-received – like when I saw Mrs Palmer in the accounts office had a twentieth wedding anniversary card on her desk and I asked her if she was bored of being married yet and she told me I was a 'cheeky little thing' – but mostly, people had been more than happy to answer my questions, and had even hung around, almost in the hope I might ask another and they could share more of their thoughts and feelings with me.

It was, I realised, exactly as Reeta had suggested: people *wanted* to be asked about themselves.

Keeping Records

The one small difficulty with my new strategy was a direct result of the way I had embarked on my mission so quickly and enthusiastically: I was receiving a huge amount of new information in a short space of time.

Over those first few days of my campaign, I found out the names of people's brothers and sisters, plans for Christmas, memories of favourite presents, favourite foods, plans for university, and stories of pets who were no longer with us.

To begin with, I was able to keep up, mostly because usually the people themselves would remind me of the details they'd previously told me, even without realising. For example, 'My dad's home tonight,' Ellie from my business class told me when I asked her what she was doing that evening. 'Meeting him at the airport.'

'Oh, is he?' I said, desperately searching my brain for whether her dad was the one in the army or the one who was setting up a pizza restaurant and going on frequent research trips to Italy.

'Yeah,' she said. 'Apparently he got some great new sauce

tips this time, so I guess we'll be eating pizza three meals a day for the next two weeks.'

Bingo. I had my answer and Ellie had no idea I'd ever faltered.

However, after one near miss when Steve the art technician told me he was going to visit his grandma as it was her birthday, I'd said, 'Oh, will you take her a present?' and he'd given me a funny look and said, 'Well, I'll put some flowers next to her headstone, I always do on important dates,' and I remembered that he'd told me just two days ago that she was dead, I realised I was going to have to get more organised.

In my field study notebook, I wrote the names of all the people I'd quizzed so far – Katie, Martin, Josh, Steve the art technician, Mrs Palmer from the office, anyone I'd spoken to at all in the last few days – at the top of a separate page, and under their name, I made a note of any facts I'd discovered so far. At the end of a conversation where new material had been gathered, I noted down the essentials on the person's page. Then, every morning, I'd just have to cast my eye over my new notes to make sure I was abreast of the key points. It did take time, as all revision does, but it was really not much to ask if it meant establishing a reputation.

One Friday morning, I was revising my notes, ready for a busy day of conversation, when Til appeared at my shoulder holding a cup of tea.

'What's that?' She nodded at my notebook.

'Just notes,' I said, trying to cover them with my arm without making them seem even more intriguing.

She pushed my hand out the way. 'Why have you got a whole page of notes on Mrs Palmer from accounts? She's like fifty. Please don't tell me you've got a thing for her now as well.'

'Ew gross, no,' I said. 'Look, I've got notes for loads of people. Not just her.' I flicked through to show her how many pages I had, how many names were listed.

Til frowned. 'What is all that?'

'It's just useful to have an *aide-memoire* sometimes. That's a memory aid, to use the English.'

'Why?'

'Because,' I said, speaking slowly like it was very obvious to anyone as socially accomplished as me, 'how will people know you care about them if you can't remember the simplest details about what they've said to you?'

'And you care about Mrs Palmer in the accounts office, do you?'

'Yes,' I said, sitting up straight and looking Til right in the eye. 'I care about everyone.'

She laughed, putting her hand over her mouth to stop the tea from escaping.

I frowned and went back to my notes. I didn't know why she always had to be so cynical about my efforts to improve myself.

'Where's my page then?' she said, nodding to the book. 'What you got written about me?'

I pulled a face. 'Well, I haven't got one for you. Obviously.'

Til's smirk faded. '"Obviously"?'

'Well, yeah. Why would I need one about you? I know all about you anyway.'

'Oh yeah, sorry. I forgot. These are only notes for people you care about.'

And then suddenly, for really no reason at all, she turned and marched out of the canteen, tossing her half-finished tea into the bin on the way.

At lunchtime, I found Reeta at our usual table in the canteen, but Til wasn't around.

'Have you seen Til today?' I asked her.

'Yeah, earlier. Why?'

'She was being properly moody this morning.'

Reeta looked up from her baked potato. 'Really?'

'Yeah. Do you know what's up with her?'

Reeta shook her head. 'She's been normal with me. But I know it's not going very well with Malcolm so maybe her mood was about that.'

'Who's Malcolm?' My first thought was that Til had somehow picked up a new boyfriend and hadn't bothered to mention it to me.

'The man she lives with, with her mum. He's got a long beard, all the way down to his belly button.'

I frowned. 'Is that a problem?'

Reeta shook her head. 'Oh no. That's not. It just surprised me. But I think it's hard for Til because she has to sleep in the porch and Malcolm comes home very late and falls over her.'

'In the porch?'

Reeta nodded but she didn't have a chance to explain any further because someone from her running club came over to ask her about meeting times and I decided I would forgive Til's outburst and ask her about her new living arrangements when I next saw her.

In Town

That Saturday, I realised there were only just over two weeks until Christmas and I hadn't done anything about getting presents for Mum or Dad or Paddy or Ollie, and I hadn't even found out if Til wanted to swap presents this year. Usually whatever I did was wrong. If I got her something, she'd say 'Why would I want that?' but if I didn't, and she'd got me something, she'd say 'Oh don't worry, I didn't expect anything from *you*,' in a pointed way, so I really couldn't win.

I was lying in bed searching online for presents so I could order it all in one go and was just considering whether a self-cleaning razor meant it cleaned *it*self or *your*self when Mum hobbled in. She was at least able to walk around the house unaided now, but she still had to move very slowly and keep her head very still and upright, like she had a metal pole running right up her back.

She put a piece of paper down on my bedside table, lowering herself to reach it by bending her knees rather than her back, like a human forklift truck.

'What's that?' I asked.

'Would you be able to go into town and get a few things for me, for Christmas? I haven't been able to do any shopping this year as I can barely walk, so I'm really behind. That's a list of everything I need.'

I picked up the list and scanned it. 'But there's basically a hundred things on here!'

'Nine.'

'Well, I'll do it online, when I've done mine. In a bit.'

Mum winced as she adjusted her position. 'I've already done the stuff I can do online. These are ones that have to be bought in person. Clothes and things.'

I stared at her, aghast. 'When am I supposed to find the time to go into town and buy one hundred and nine things for you when I've got college and a job and a business to run?'

'I thought you said the business wasn't going to interfere with A levels.'

When I'd told Mum and Dad about the addition of Bashed to my life, they went on and on about being worried it was going to become 'one of my obsessions' and interfere with college. 'You know what you're like, Grace,' Mum had said, unsupportively. 'You get a bee in your bonnet and you think about nothing else. So I don't know if it's a good idea you get involved with a new project when you've only really just started your A levels.'

'It's fine,' I told her. 'Kendall and Molly have been managing it fine for years. I'm only doing a little bit of it. And it will look really good on my CV. Working for a real, actual business is way better than just having a business studies A level.'

'That's true,' Dad had said, and Mum had looked like she

might say something else but in the end she just held her hands up and said, 'OK, OK,' and went to unload the dishwasher.

'Well, it's not interfering with A levels,' I told Mum now. 'It is interfering with being your slave and I never promised I'd have time for that.'

'Grace,' Mum said, her voice cross now. 'It's not being my slave, it's doing me a favour when I'm not very well. Please be helpful.'

'Fine,' I said. 'I'll get it when I go into town later to get the presents for the Santa party.'

My costume for my role as Santa at Marie's Christmas party was finished, but I still needed to go out and buy twenty presents for each of Marie's friends. All of them had to be found for five pounds or less and all had to be 'quirky, interesting or useful – preferably all three'.

Marie had told Kendall that she wanted to show each of her friends how much they personally meant to her and apparently the best way she could think of to do that was to send a sixteen-year-old she'd met once to choose and wrap the presents.

I headed into town with my empty hiking rucksack on my back. I had hoped to be able to put all twenty items in it and do the whole lot in one go but with Mum's nine presents on the list too, it looked like I would have to do two trips.

The shopping was going as well as could be expected and I had managed to pick up several of the Santa presents in a new homeware shop that sold things you would never have thought you needed until you saw them:

A torch shaped like an ice cream.

A plastic bear that danced when your phone rang.

A miniature dartboard for the back of the toilet door.

I was just wrestling my purchases into my rucksack and realising I was going to have to head home shortly for a drop-off when I heard a familiar voice behind me. 'Oh my god, babe, no!'

I turned around and saw Kendall, Molly and two other girls from the Booth bundled up in big coats and scarves sitting on some metal chairs outside a cafe. Kendall was looking at something on one of the other girls' phones and laughing loudly and shaking her head.

Seeing Kendall unexpectedly, out and about and not in one of the places I was used to seeing her, like her house or in college, made my heart beat quicker. I was a bit annoyed because I had given myself several stern talkings-to about this. I'd admitted to myself that although perhaps I did like her a little more than just as friends, it was only a little bit, and as nothing would ever, ever, ever happen in a million years for a million reasons (like she liked boys and particularly obviously still this one 'Eddie' boy in Scotland) I had put the whole idea out of my head.

'Hey,' I said, turning around to stand at the edge of their table. I was suddenly aware my rucksack made me look like I was a mountaineer. Or a tortoise.

Kendall looked up, surprised.

'Oh, hey, Gracie,' she said.

She pulled out a chair and nodded to it in silent invitation. I sat down, and she immediately went back to her conversation as if she'd been expecting me all along.

I gathered they were talking about a holiday they were going on and how someone I hadn't heard of had dropped out, which meant that all of them were going to have to pay more for the house they were staying in.

'It drives me crazy,' Molly said, her eyes fixed on her phone as usual. 'Like, why say you're going to do something if you're not going to? It's just selfish.'

'I know,' one of the other girls agreed. 'And why not tell us a bit sooner? We're never going to find someone else now.'

'Unless . . .' Kendall said. She peered at me, her head on one side, twisting a strand of hair around her finger. 'Grace? You up for it?'

'Huh?' I said. 'Up for what?'

'Coming with!' she said. 'To the house!'

'What house?'

'OK,' Kendall said, turning her chair around so she was talking to me head-on. 'So we go to this cottage every year. It's in the countryside and it's really nice and I used to go there when I was a kid so now the owners let us have it cheap as it's off season. It's got a hot tub.'

'A hot tub?' I repeated. I had been in the jacuzzi at the gym Mum went to before but never a private one, in a house I was staying in. And never with Kendall.

'Yeah!' Kendall said. 'And a stereo and a big TV so we just, like, chill and catch up. Watch films. Because life can get mental, you know?

'Oh,' I said. 'Yes, mental. With all the parties and everything.'

'Exactly,' Kendall said. 'We just need some down time. So what do you reckon? You in?'

I hesitated, blinking stupidly. One minute I'd been walking along doing my Christmas shopping, now here I was, being invited on an actual holiday with Kendall and Molly and two girls who I only knew by sight and couldn't even name.

I surely could not actually go.

Could I?

'Oh yeah, definitely!' I said, nodding and smiling in a way that tried to convey that I was totally relaxed about this situation.

There was a lot I hadn't had time to think about:

What would Mum and Dad say about this spontaneous holiday?

So far I'd only spoken to Kendall in short doses, for half an hour here and there – would I be able to be witty and charming and *nice* for a whole weekend?

What should I take? How would we get there?

But I decided to think through the details later. It was too exciting an opportunity to turn down.

Skinned Alive

Later that evening, I arrived at Reeta's with a Boots carrier bag tucked away safely at the bottom of my rucksack.

'Hey!' she said brightly when she opened the door. She smiled and took a bite of her peanut butter toast, as if I was there for a perfectly casual and ordinary social call.

'Hello,' I said grimly.

She laughed. 'Your face!'

I didn't respond. I just said, 'Shall I go up?' and nodded up the stairs towards her bedroom.

'Yeah. Two secs. I'll just –'

But she was cut off by the voice of her mum calling from the kitchen. 'Reeta, have you got any more lights before I put this load on?'

I froze and looked at her wide-eyed. 'Your *mum's* here?'

Reeta nodded, still appearing absurdly casual about the whole thing. 'Yeah, but everyone else is out.'

'Reeta!' I stared at her. 'You said EVERYONE would be out! Not everyone-except-your-mum. Who, no offence but, spends a lot of time walking around the house and in and out of rooms including your room!'

'It's fine,' Reeta said, shaking her head and putting her hand on my arm to calm me. 'Don't worry.'

Just then her mum, Gloria, came out of the kitchen. 'Oh, hi, Grace,' she said. 'What have you girls got planned for the evening?'

I was about to step in and say something about a science project we needed to work on together – although lord knows why when neither of us were even taking science – when Reeta said, 'Grace wants me to wax her legs. So we'll be in my bedroom and you're not to come in at all, OK, because she's very embarrassed about it.'

'Reeta!' I hissed.

'Relax,' Reeta said, with a wave of her hand. 'She doesn't care. No one cares.'

Reeta's mum didn't even look up from her phone. She did indeed seem to be completely uninterested in the news. 'Rather you than me, love,' she muttered before wandering into the lounge.

It had been Reeta's suggestion that I got a full leg wax before I went on my hot-tub cottage retreat. Or at least, it was her who had put the idea in my head that it might be a sensible precaution.

I had been telling Reeta about the trip, and specifically about the exciting hot tub element, when it had occurred to me. 'Oh god, I suppose I'm going to have to shave my legs. Right up to the top! I best get started soon, it can take me several days to get through it all. There's a lot of surface area to cover.'

'I'll do you a wax if you like,' Reeta had said. 'It'll last longer. That's what all the girls at swimming do.'

I peered at her then down at my legs. 'Wax my . . . put wax . . . on my legs? All over?'

I knew that was something people did, but I always thought it was for the type of people who got their eyebrows plucked by professionals and who knew the difference between cleanser and toner, i.e., not for people like me.

Reeta laughed. 'Yep.'

'I don't know,' I said. 'I don't know about that. I'm not really a leg wax kind of person. It's meant to hurt a lot, isn't it? And I am particularly sensitive to pain. I haven't had a formal diagnosis, but I wouldn't be surprised to find out I have three times as many nerve endings in my skin than everyone else.'

Reeta shrugged. 'I don't think it hurts that much. It's fast. I'll do it for you, then you don't have to look. You can just sit still for three minutes and then . . . whoosh! All done.'

So there I was, standing in Reeta's hall with a box of cold wax strips in my rucksack ready for her to take me to her room and skin me alive. Or near enough.

I followed Reeta upstairs like a prisoner being led to the electric chair. I stood in the middle of her bedroom and waited until she'd shut the door.

'Take your trousers off then,' she said, gesturing to my jeans.

I hesitated.

Reeta sighed. 'Listen, Gracie, if you're going to be getting in a hot tub you're going to have to be getting your clothes

169

off. And that will be in front of Kendall, who you love. So you better practise now.

'I don't love her!' I protested. 'I barely know her! She's just a colleague.'

Reeta didn't reply but I knew she had a point. I needed to loosen up or forget the idea of going at all. I peeled off my jeans and lay, as directed, on her bed.

Reeta was very professional about the whole business, directing me where to lie and how to bend my legs, as she placed a wax strip on my shin and smoothed it down.

'OK,' she said when it was firmly attached. 'Hold tight, it'll be over in a flash.'

'No!' I shouted suddenly.

She froze. 'What?'

'I can't face it,' I said quietly. 'I'm not ready.'

She frowned. 'Well, it's on now.' We both looked down at the strip.

'Just leave it there,' I said.

'Gracie! I can't just leave it there!'

'Just for a while,' I said. 'I mean, why don't you put all of the strips on first. Then when my legs are all covered, we can take them all off in one go and get it over with.'

Reeta frowned. 'I'm not sure you can do it like that.'

'Please,' I said. 'I'm just not quite ready. I need a little more time.'

Reeta sighed again but began sticking the strips of wax-covered papers to the fronts and backs of my legs until they were completely covered. When I looked down I had the feeling I was wearing a pair of patchwork paper leggings.

'Now,' she said eventually. 'We'll have to take them off.'

I nodded and looked up at the ceiling. I felt her take hold of one wax strip, and pull the skin on my leg tight underneath.

'No!' I shouted again. I sat up, pulling my leg away from her grasp. 'I can't, Reeta. You can't. I can't go through with it. It was a mistake to ever think I could.'

'Gracie!' Reeta said, exasperated now. 'It's too late to change your mind. The wax is on. It has to come off again.'

'So just . . . peel it off gently,' I said, pulling carefully at one of the corners. 'Just skip the ripping part. Peel it off slowly and carefully.'

'But then the hair won't come off! You have to rip to pull the hair out from the root! That's how it works!'

It sounded so brutal when she put it like that that I don't know why on earth I had agreed to the idea in the first place.

'I don't care!' I said. I was starting to feel a bit panicked by my paper patchwork trousers, like the strips were smothering me alive and I needed to escape. 'I don't care about the hair, just get it off me!'

'OK, OK. Calm down.'

Very gently she began peeling each of the wax strips away from my skin. That alone was quite painful enough so I was left in no doubt that if I'd gone ahead with the full procedure I would be unconscious by now. Or dead.

'Well', Reeta said uncertainly fifteen minutes later, a pile of paper strips on the floor next to her bed. 'The paper's off. But the wax is trickier.'

I sat up and looked at my legs. The entire surface of my

skin was covered in a gloopy, patchy layer of blue wax, right from my ankle to the top of my thighs.

'Will it wash off?' I asked.

Reeta winced and shook her head. 'Not with water. I don't know. I've never seen this much left on before. It's like you've got a second skin.' She shrugged helplessly.

'Well, never mind,' I said breezily, climbing to my feet and reaching for my jeans. 'I can live with it. It's probably good for me. Moisturising or protective or something. And I'm sure it will work its way off eventually. My skin will probably grow and push it –'

'Grace, no,' Reeta said, taking my jeans out of my hand. 'You can't put your trousers on over it! They'll get stuck to it and then you'll have to wear those trousers for the rest of your life!'

I stopped and looked down. 'Well, what shall I do?' I was starting to feel panicked again. I really wished I'd never come.

Reeta thought for a moment. Then she said, 'Wait here,' and left her room before I could point out that I wasn't really likely to be going anywhere, in my current state.

A minute later she returned, and right behind her was her mum.

'Argh!' I screamed and tried to hide behind Reeta's desk.

Gloria simply followed me and stood there looking down at my legs. 'Don't worry, love. It's nothing I haven't seen before. Especially in my line of work.'

'Aren't you a vet?' I said.

She ignored my question. 'I'll get some oil,' she said.

A few minutes later and I was back in position on Reeta's

bed while Reeta, her mum and I carefully rubbed at the patches of blue wax with cotton-wool balls soaked in baby oil.

'It's ridiculous, you know,' Gloria said. 'The boys don't bother with any of this, do they? They just leave their legs exactly as they are. Really, all it takes is for one girl not to bother and then all the rest of you would realise you didn't have to either.'

'Well, it looks like I'm going to be that one girl, doesn't it,' I said grumpily.

'I think that's a good thing,' Reeta said. 'Kendall isn't going to not like you just because you have hair on your legs. That's like not liking you because you breathe air or eat food. And she's not that kind of person, is she?'

I shook my head, but really I wasn't totally sure what kind of person Kendall was at all.

Road Trip

As I had suspected, Mum and Dad weren't particularly enthusiastic about the idea of me going on an impromptu weekend away with a group of girls they'd never met and had only begun mentioning at all in the last few weeks.

'This is the first I've heard of it,' Mum said when I told her of the plan, the day after my waxing disaster.

'Well, I only heard of it myself a few days ago. It's just a spur of the moment type thing. Someone pulled out.'

'So you're just going to make up the numbers?' Ollie said with a smirk. 'What an honour.'

'No, Oliver,' I told him slowly, 'I'm going because they want me to, and I want to, and because now there's room for me. Which there wasn't before because they didn't even know me to know that I would want to come and that they would want me to come.'

'They do seem to have sprung up from nowhere,' Mum said. 'These new friends. And now you're spending all your time with them? Why don't you go away with Til and Reeta instead?'

'Because Til and Reeta aren't going away! And it's hardly all my time. We're running a business together, that's all.'

I could see Mum thinking of something else annoying to say so I jumped in before she could.

'Look, I've already said I'll go and if I don't then it will mess up all the numbers and the money and no one will be able to go. It's for one night and it's only about half an hour away. It's really no more of a big deal than when I stay the night at Til's or Reeta's.'

Mum shook her head and sighed like she was tired of the whole thing, which is what I'd been aiming for. 'Fine, fine. What about work though? You won't be back in time to start your shift at nine, surely?'

'I've taken the day off.'

Leonard was less than pleased at the idea of me taking a random day off two weeks before Christmas but as I saw it, if things continued to go well with Bashed, hopefully I would be able to stop working at Podrick's altogether before too long.

I reported to Kendall's drive at eleven on Saturday morning as detailed in the message she'd sent me with the arrangements. The doors of Kendall's little blue car were open and Molly and the two girls who'd been outside the cafe were standing alongside it holding wheelie suitcases like the type pilots and people who go on business trips use that made my purple camping rucksack feel very unsophisticated.

'Oh, hey, Grace,' Molly said, looking up briefly before continuing to shuffle bags in the boot.

'Hey.' I stood back from them, feeling self-conscious.

When I'd agreed to come on the trip outside the cafe the week before, Kendall had formally introduced me to the other members of our group. They were called Jules and Dog. ('Her real name's Cat, but we call her Dog,' Molly had explained.) but I didn't know much more about them than that. I had told myself I was OK with going on a mini-break with virtual strangers but now I was here, with my bag packed, facing them, I felt a bit nervous.

Kendall emerged from the house, pulling her own wheelie suitcase behind her, her hair piled on top of her head in the trademark cool way that I tried so many times to copy but only ever ended up looking like I was wearing a comedy hat.

'Oh, hi, Grace,' she said, flashing me one of her wide but slightly surprised smiles. She often did those, I'd noticed. They gave me the feeling that she wasn't expecting to find me there but wasn't unhappy that I was. 'Let's get this show on the road!'

She climbed into the driver's seat. Dog pulled open the passenger door and climbed in. For a moment I hovered next to the car, not sure what to do.

The previous evening, I had messaged Kendall.

**Me: One small thing – is it OK if I sit in the front?
I get properly car sick in the back**

Kendall: Course babe x

But it looked like no one had shared the detail of this agreement with Dog. I realised Kendall had probably forgotten all about it, so I was going to have to say something if I didn't want to arrive at the cottage feeling like I'd been on a spin cycle in a washing machine.

'Um, Dog . . .' I said, hovering next to the passenger side of the car.

She looked up at me questioningly but didn't say anything. I realised I hadn't heard her say anything out loud at all yet. I wondered if she ever did. Maybe she barked.

'It's just . . . Kendall said it would be OK if I sat up front because I get really car sick in the back. Like seriously car sick, honestly.' I laughed and shook my head as if to show I knew it was a ridiculous situation but there was nothing I could do about it.

She peered at me curiously, but she didn't get up from her seat.

I had hoped that Kendall, having been reminded of my request, would chip in and get her to move, but she was checking her lipstick in the wing mirror and acting like she couldn't hear the conversation at all.

Dog made a kind of wincing face, crinkling up her nose. Then finally she spoke, 'Thing is though, music, you know?'

She held up her phone and I looked at it, confused.

Molly leant forward. 'Dog is official road-trip DJ. She always is.'

'Oh.' I blinked. 'OK, sure. I mean, I can still play your music in the front. Or I've got music on my phone or –'

Dog did the wincing face again and shook her head. 'Sorry,' she said simply, and pulled the door shut.

Kendall laughed. 'Dog, you're such a moody cow.'

But Dog just shrugged and Kendall showed no sign of stepping in to enforce our agreement.

I stood by the side of the car not knowing what to do. I considered my options. Should I open the door and plead my case again? Should I ask Kendall for support? Should I tell them I'd make my own way there on the train? There was part of me that suddenly wanted to forget the whole idea of the trip altogether. I found this Dog-Cat girl a bit intimidating and I wasn't sure I wanted to be friends with her, despite her Booth status. But I took a moment and made myself appreciate how far I'd come in a short time. Just a few weeks ago, I hadn't even been able to get an invite to an ordinary party by an ordinary and actually quite annoying boy like Jon-Jon. Now, here I was, in the inner circle, going on a weekend away with half the Booth.

I remembered then what had carried me this far: my personal brand. My niceness. That was what Kendall had liked about me. How nice would I look if I started getting stroppy now about where I sat in the car?

'Come and sit in the middle,' Molly called from the back seat. 'Then you can look through the front and you won't get sick.'

I knew from bitter experience that this was in no way true, but I also knew I didn't have any choice.

'Oh OK,' I said brightly, like this was a wonderful idea that had never before occurred to me. 'That should work.'

Molly got out to make way for me and I took my seat in the middle of the back seat, squashed up next to Jules and the large leopard-print bag she'd decided to hold on her lap like it was a pet, and we were ready to go.

'Don't worry, Gracie,' Kendall said. 'It's only a short drive.'

Then she caught my eye in the rear-view mirror and gave me a wink, and suddenly I didn't really care where I sat.

The Hideaway

The drive was not short.

Kendall had been vague about the location, mentioning only 'about half an hour', 'a few miles' and 'London-ish way' but as I watched the motorway slip past with no sign of Kendall turning off I realised I had no idea where we were. By the time we'd navigated some winding country lanes and arrived in the driveway of a small but smart house with a wooden sign reading 'The Hideaway' we had been in the car nearly two hours, and I was feeling very sick and very exhausted from keeping my mouth clamped tight shut so I wouldn't puke all over the car and everyone in it.

As the doors of the car were thrown open and we all tumbled out I stood in the middle of the driveway taking deep breaths of cold country air and swaying slightly as I waited for my spinning head to calm down.

'See? Wasn't so bad, was it?' Molly said, slapping me on the back and nearly knocking me over. I forced myself to smile.

Kendall opened the heavy wooden door to the house and we took our bags inside.

'Hello, old friend,' Jules said, looking around at the entrance hall.

Even through my nausea, I could see the place was impressive. It wasn't really a cottage at all, but a converted barn with a huge fireplace in the middle, sofas surrounding it and one wall made entirely of glass – through which I could see the decking area, complete with a dazzling view of the hills and the infamous hot tub.

I sat down on a sofa and looked out. 'Wow,' I said. 'Amazing.'

'Isn't it?' Kendall said, coming over to me. She draped her arm over my shoulder and I sat up very still, not sure what I should do and not wanting to get it wrong.

'OK!' Kendall said, slapping her knees and standing up. 'Supplies run!'

The other three groaned.

'Oh, come on,' Kendall said. 'The supermarket is like ten minutes away. We can be back within the hour, then we can hit the tub.'

'I'm not going,' Dog said simply, slouching in the corner of a sofa.

'Yeah, I don't want to go back in the car right now,' Jules said. 'Let's do it later.'

Molly didn't say anything at all. Her eyes, as ever, were firmly on her phone.

Kendall sighed. 'Fine, me and Grace will do it.'

I was about to point out, politely, that if I got back in the car there was a good chance my whole stomach might explode, when Kendall added, 'At least I can count on *one* of my friends to actually help me out,' and put her arm around my shoulders again.

Aside from the sickness issue, I realised that it might actually be fun to go on a little outing, just me and Kendall. I almost never saw her on her own. And at least this time I'd be able to sit in the front.

At the supermarket, I pushed the trolley and Kendall walked ahead of me, pulling things from the shelves as frantically as if we were expecting a zombie invasion and therefore planning to hide out in the cottage for the next five years.

She'd asked us all to put twenty pounds in a little red purse she'd brought with her for 'provisions', which had seemed a bit much to me, but I could see now that Kendall didn't like to be restricted when she was shopping.

We didn't talk much on the way back to the cottage, Kendall quietly singing along with the radio, but as we turned off the main road and began to trundle slowly down the lane to the house, she put her hand on my leg and said, 'I'm so glad you've come, Gracie.'

I felt my cheeks glow. 'Oh,' I said. 'Me too.'

'I mean, because the thing is – and do not tell the others – but I've been having kind of a hard time with Eddie this week.'

'As in, your ex, Eddie? In Scotland?'

She nodded. 'Like, Molly knows he texts me occasionally but actually this week we've spoken on the phone like every night. For two hours last night!'

'What about? If he's your ex?'

Kendall sighed. 'I dunno. It's kind of complicated. He says he doesn't want to get back with me because he wants to be single at university, but then he says he still loves me . . . and . . .' She sighed again. 'I don't know. That's part of the reason why I want it to work out with Bashed so much. Because if I can show him that I'm not just some immature kid, that I can run a business even better than he could, maybe he'll . . .' She trailed off. 'I don't know. I'm an idiot, aren't I?'

I shook my head. 'No. Not at all.' Although the truth was, I thought she was a bit, at least about this. But not as much as I thought this Eddie was an idiot, not only for ditching someone like Kendall in the first place, but for carrying on messing with her afterwards.

'You're lucky, you know,' she said.

'How do you mean?'

'Going out with girls.'

'Oh,' I said. 'That.'

I was surprised. It wasn't a secret and lots of people at college knew that Sarah in the year above had been my girlfriend for about six weeks until I managed to totally mess it up, but Kendall had never made reference to it before.

'I mean, I don't know if I can say I go out with girls. I went out with one, once. Who knows if I'll ever find another one.'

'Oh, you will,' she said. She put her hand on my leg again. 'You definitely will.'

'Thanks for your confidence,' I said, turning away from her to look out the window so she couldn't see how much I was blushing.

'Maybe I'll give it a go myself sometime.'

I did look at her then. 'Girls?'

She laughed. 'Why not?'

I wasn't sure what to make of it. What was she trying to say?

I wanted her to go on but we were pulling into the drive, and then the doors were open and the others had come to check out what we'd bought and the moment was over.

My Best Self

Having sat in the back for the whole awful two-hour drive in order to show just how nice I could be, I didn't want to waste any good impression I had made by letting the act slip now.

I realised that here, on this weekend away, I had a prime opportunity to show myself at my best. But it was going to take some effort.

As we climbed out of the car, I turned to Kendall and said, 'Why don't you go and chill out? You must be tired from all the driving. I can bring the shopping in.'

Kendall closed her eyes briefly. Then she nodded and made for the door. 'You are such an angel!' she called back.

Inside, the others were still slouching on the sofa pretty much exactly where I'd left them, and once the shopping was unpacked, I said, to no one in particular, 'I guess I should put my own stuff away . . . which bedroom is mine?'

I hadn't had a chance to fully explore of the house yet, but there were three doors off the lounge so I assumed each one was a bedroom. I hoped that Kendall and I might end up sharing and we could talk, just the two of us, late into the night and she might tell me again how glad she was I'd come and how I was the only one to truly understand her struggles.

'Oh, you're on the sofa bed, hun,' Kendall said from the corner where she was busy fiddling with the stereo.

'Sofa bed? Where?'

'Uh,' Kendall looked around the room vaguely. 'That one, I think.' She pointed at the sofa Dog was currently sprawled across. 'There are only four beds, so as you're the newcomer . . . it's kind of a first-come, first-served thing, you know?'

I paused for just the briefest of moments, but then I said, 'Oh, OK. That's cool. That's fine. I can sleep anywhere.'

I realised that as Dog was currently occupying my bed I would just have to leave my bag where it was, by the front door.

So instead I said, 'Can I get anyone a drink?'

With no room of my own to retreat to, I decided I might as well press on with my niceness mission. It's just twenty-four hours, I told myself. And if I played it right and kept it up the whole time, this could be the weekend that marked the transition between my life as a no one and my life as a someone. A nice, popular someone.

This weekend was my formal audition for the role and I was going to give it my best.

Nice Grace Mark Two

Over the next four hours, Nice Grace went into overdrive. I was Nice Grace Mark Two with added Niceness and Amenability and an expansion pack of Heartfelt Compliments.

I began my efforts with the catering. This seemed an easy way in. It started with a round of Cokes, progressed through to bowls of popcorn, two plates of toast and Marmite and, for Jules, a fried egg sandwich with ketchup spread on one piece of bread and mustard spread on the other because, 'That's how Mum always does it and I'm kind of missing her to be honest.'

'Is she away?' I said, wondering, for some reason, if she was in prison.

Jules frowned. 'No. I am. I'm here? Normally Mum brings me food, like, all day. We're really close.'

'Oh. OK.' I wondered if I should feel bad that I wasn't missing my own mum but then it had only been a few hours. I decided Mum probably wasn't missing me yet either.

The supply of food was just the beginning.

187

Over the course of the afternoon, I plumped cushions, plugged phones into chargers, scoured the barn for a hairdryer for Molly and hauled duvets out of bedrooms and laid them over cold legs. When Kendall asked me to get her slippers from her bag, I didn't just bring them to her, but crouched down and slipped them onto her feet. When Dog, who was sitting painting her nails, said, 'Grace, do us a favour, would you, and get my deodorant out of my bag,' not only did I fetch it, but I didn't even pause when she said, 'My nails are still wet, can you spray?' and lifted her arms and I was forced to spray her armpits like I was doing a very strange graffiti project.

We basically did nothing for the whole afternoon. Personally, I was thinking that if all we were going to do was lie on separate sofas, looking at our phones with music on in the background, with Dog changing the song after twenty seconds of each one, we might as well have saved ourselves the money and stayed at home and done this in one of our bedrooms.

But I had to remind myself that if that had been the case, I probably wouldn't have been with them at all. I had never been invited to hang out with them at the weekend. But I *had* been invited on this trip. I had to hold on to that.

At one point, Kendall disappeared into her bedroom and when she hadn't emerged ten minutes or so later, I decided to go to check if she was OK.

I found her sitting on her bed, staring forlornly at her phone in her lap.

'Are you OK?' I asked quietly.

She nodded but she was chewing on her lip.

'Did Eddie call? What happened?'

She shook her head. 'No. No call. No message. Nothing happened.'

I nodded wisely. 'Ah. I see. And sometimes nothing is the worst.'

She closed her eyes. 'Yeah.'

I went and sat next to her and thought about what to do. It seemed a good time for a hug, but so far she had been the one to initiate them all and I didn't want to get it wrong. In the end, I didn't have to make the decision because she pulled me close to her and said into my neck, 'Why are boys so stressful!' and I rubbed her back and said, 'I don't know, I don't know,' because I didn't.

Then she pulled away and stood up and smoothed down her top. She took a tissue from the dresser and blew her nose. Then she fixed me with one of her intense looks and said, 'I think we'll be friends for ever now, you and me. Don't you?'

I nodded firmly. 'Yes. Definitely.'

My stomach felt like the rollercoaster hadn't so much hit the downhill bit as flown right off the track.

Not-So-Hot Tub

As the afternoon drifted into the evening, attention turned to the subject of going in the hot tub and the others went to their rooms to change into their swimming gear. I held back though, partly because I didn't have a bedroom to go to, and partly because I'd been growing increasingly unsure about whether getting my clothes off with these girls was really a good idea.

I had brought my swimming costume – the one I'd bought when I decided to get into swimming the year before, but had only used once after a plaster had drifted into my mouth on my first trip to the pool and I'd vowed never to go back. It wasn't a terrible costume – plain black, functional – but with the others discussing which bikinis they'd brought and Molly saying hers had been based on a design Kim Kardashian had worn on a trip to Honolulu, I realised how I'd look standing next to them.

'You coming in then, Gracie?' Kendall asked as I watched them all sashay across the barn in their bikinis, their skin smooth and perfectly tanned – *how* exactly were they so tanned when it was December? – and I thought about my own legs, scabby where I had shaved them with Ollie's blunt razor, furry in the patches where I'd got bored and couldn't reach the back and, in a few places, still sticky with blue wax.

I had imagined that they might find it funny, what a mess I'd made. I thought Kendall might even find it endearing somehow. But looking at them all now, I realised I was just gross.

'Nah,' I said. 'I'm not really into water. I'll just watch.'

Dog gave me a funny look and pulled her robe around her to shield herself. 'Watch?'

'Oh!' I forced myself to laugh. 'I just mean, you know. Sit and talk. Not go in.'

Dog nodded, heaved open the sliding glass doors that led to the deck and slipped into the hot tub. I followed them out and sat on a plastic chair on the edge, but the noise from the bubbles made it hard for me to hear what they were saying and they weren't really talking to me anyway. I looked enviously at the steam rising from the hot water and shivered, pulling my hoody around me. In the end, I gave up and went inside and watched them from the sofa though the window.

I hoped that Kendall might get bored and come in on her own to talk to me about Eddie – about anything – and tell me again how she knew we'd be friends for life, but she didn't show any signs of getting bored and before long I started to get tired. It had been a busy day of fetching, carrying and making food and I just wanted my bed. The only problem was, my bed was in the lounge, which right now was brightly lit with the main lounge lights, which they needed on to be able to see outside, and noisy with the music they'd turned up to be able to hear over the bubbles.

There was no way I was going to be able to sleep on the sofa with all that going on. I looked wistfully towards the bedrooms and wished I had one of my own to escape to. In the end, I went over to the room Kendall and Molly were sharing and stood in the doorway looking at their clean, soft beds.

I could just lie down in there, couldn't I? I could get some rest and some peace from the noise and the light, and when Molly and Kendall returned and it was time for lights out I could take my place on the sofa bed.

I lay down on Kendall's bed, just on top of the covers, and looked up at the ceiling. I was exhausted, I realised. And suddenly, so cold. Outside, I heard a whooping noise and a laugh and then the sound of Kendall's voice saying, 'Oh my god, what are you like!'

They would be out there for hours, I was sure. I pulled the duvet back and climbed under, just for a moment, just to warm up. I still had no intention of actually sleeping there.

The next thing I knew the light had been flicked on and Kendall was standing over me, frowning, and Molly was sniggering in the corner behind, one hand over her mouth. 'Uh, Grace, that's my bed?' Kendall said. Her head was on one side like she found the sight of me truly confusing.

I looked up at her for a moment, trying to work out why Kendall and Molly were in my room and why they were waking me up in the middle of the night. Then I realised that it wasn't my room at all, it was their room, and I hastily pushed myself upright and tried to disentangle my legs from the duvet.

'Sorry. So sorry,' I said groggily. 'I was just resting. I didn't mean . . .'

'Ew, Gracie, you've dribbled on her pillow,' Molly said, picking up the pillow and holding it out in front of her like it had been splashed with toxic waste.

'Sorry,' I said, wiping my mouth with the back of my hand. As cold as I'd been when I went to sleep I now felt sweaty and dirty and I knew I must look a mess. What had I been thinking, getting into Kendall's bed?

I scrambled out of the bed and stood guiltily in the middle of the room like a toddler awaiting a smacking.

'There's a blanket in the cupboard under the TV,' Kendall said with a yawn, taking my place in her bed.

I realised this was my cue to leave the room, and as I shut the door behind me, I heard Molly giggle and whisper, 'I told you she fancied you!'

I didn't hang around to hear Kendall's reply.

Bad Night

I did not sleep well that night.

The blanket was one of those old-fashioned woollen ones and was scratchy against my skin and there was no pillow anywhere to be found. Also, Kendall's description of a sofa bed turned out to be only half true, in that it *was* a sofa and also my bed for the night, but really it was just a sofa. And not really one long enough for a full-sized human such as myself to lie on comfortably.

I couldn't stop thinking about what had just happened in the bedroom. Why had Molly said that? What had Kendall replied? Was Molly jealous, thinking I might be taking her place as Kendall's special, number-one friend?

I had so many thoughts in my head and it was so cold in the open-plan barn that it was only sometime after 3 a.m. that I managed to get to sleep.

At 7 a.m. the others started to wake up and stumble out of their rooms and into mine.

'Let's have pancakes,' Molly said, grabbing a plastic bowl and beginning to throw ingredients in, sloshing milk all over the work surface. I winced, feeling quite sure it would be my job to clear that up later. I wondered if this is what it felt like to be a parent.

Kendall came out of her room wearing her robe and I could see from the pink tie at the back of her neck she had her bikini on.

'Just going for a quick dip before breakfast,' Kendall said.

Molly and Jules were busy in the kitchen and there was no sign of Dog yet, so partly because I wasn't sure what to do with myself and partly because I liked it when Kendall and I were alone, I said, 'I'll come and keep you company.'

Kendall paused and looked at me for a moment, then she said, 'Gracie, could we have a little talk?'

I blinked. 'Oh . . . yeah? OK?'

She sat down on the sofa and patted the seat next to her, indicating I should join her. I wasn't sure why she couldn't have just come to the sofa I was already on but I obediently went over anyway.

'You know I really like you and everything,' she began.

'I like you too,' I said. 'Loads.'

I immediately wished I hadn't added the 'loads'. It sounded too much, and Kendall obviously thought so too, judging by the face she was pulling.

'Yeah,' she said.

'Yeah?' I asked. I really had no idea where this was going.

'I do really want to be good friends with you, Gracie. You're so cool and just so . . . nice? Have I ever told you how nice you are?'

I nodded. 'Yeah.'

'It's just . . . I mean, I don't want to sound massively up myself or whatever but I do want to be honest here . . . I'm just not into girls, you know? I mean, I wish I was sometimes . . . but it's just not for me.'

'Oh, I know!' I said quickly. 'You've got Eddie, sort of, and –'

Kendall cut me off. 'It's just last night was a bit . . . surprising. To find you in my bed, I mean. I didn't want you to think you could just climb in and when I got back I'd . . .'

'Oh, I didn't think anything!' I said. 'Honestly, I was just tired and wanted to lie down in a bed. That is literally all.'

Kendall looked like she was going to say something else or ask another question, but in the end she just nodded and said. 'OK. If you're sure.'

'Honestly, Kendall,' I said. 'I do like you but only as a friend.'

I wasn't sure that was true, but it was definitely the right thing to say.

'And really, I'm not over my ex, Sarah, so I'm not into anyone right now.'

I wasn't sure that was true either. I certainly didn't think much about Sarah when Kendall was around.

Kendall nodded again.

We sat looking at each other awkwardly for a moment. Then she said, 'Hug it out?' and pulled me into one of her tight squeezes.

When we let go, she said. 'So we're cool?'

'Yeah!' I said, a little too loudly. 'Absolutely!'

She smiled. She seemed genuinely relived. 'Cool. Because you really are special to me, Gracie.'

I smiled. Being special was good enough for me.

PART 4:

Where I am hospitalised by a dog in a Venetian mask

Focus

On the Sunday evening, after we'd returned from the house, Mum wanted me to join them for a family dinner so I could tell them all about my 'adventure', like I'd been on a camping expedition with the Girl Guides, but I really didn't feel like sitting there and telling them all about what had happened with the hot tub and the bed mix-up and Molly making Kendall think I fancied her.

I just wanted to be on my own, so I retreated to my bed with my notebook.

As I looked back over the notes I'd made when I first set out to increase my popularity a few weeks ago, I realised that, somewhere along the way, things had got a bit muddled.

The problem was, I'd been chasing too many things. I wanted too much. I wanted to be popular. I wanted people to like me. I also wanted to be nice, partly to get people to like me but, I was realising, partly because it felt good to be a good person. And if being nice meant that I became popular too, then that was a win-win situation, wasn't it?

But then, as a related but really quite separate issue, there was Kendall. And that's where things had got tricky. I'd got too attached to her, I knew.

When I was trying to impress her because she was the leader of the Booth and one of the most popular people in college, it made sense. Being friends with Kendall was simply a good strategy. However, I needed to let go of any feelings I had for her. She said she liked me and that was all I could hope for from her. We had already peaked. I needed to keep my emotions in check and focus on the task in hand.

There were just three days of college to get through until the Christmas holidays. When I arrived at college on Monday, I found Mac standing on a stepladder, fiddling with a bulb on the Christmas lights that were looped across the ceiling at reception.

'Hey, Gracie!' he called, cheery as ever.

'Oh, hi, Mac,' I said, stopping to look up.

He climbed down the ladder. 'You all ready for Christmas then?'

'Yeah,' I said. 'Yeah, I guess. You?'

He sighed. 'It's going to be different this year, that's for sure.'

'Ah, yeah. Of course. With the fire and everything.'

He nodded sadly. 'Yeah. We normally have it all – two trees, all the decs, everyone over – but this year we'll be stuck in a B & B until we get ourselves sorted. No tree, obviously. We've got a little cactus and Mrs Mac's tied a ribbon round it. Won't be much of a celebration this year though.'

'No,' I said. Even Mac couldn't put a positive spin on things this time.

'Still,' he said, reaching for a screwdriver from his toolbox, 'hoping to start getting back on our feet in the New Year.'

'You know,' I began. 'We're trying to help you . . . me and Kendall and Molly.'

I wasn't sure if anyone had actually told Mac about our plans to donate our profits to him. I thought maybe it was better we didn't, before we knew exactly how much that might be – better to keep it as a nice surprise. Now though, I thought the news might cheer him up.

He smiled then. 'Yeah,' he said quietly. 'Someone did mention that. Bless ya hearts.'

'Maybe that'll help a bit?' I said hopefully.

He nodded. 'Maybe! No pressure though, on you kids. You're doing the best you can, I'm sure,' and then he climbed back up his ladder and resumed his repairs.

Eight Hundred Pounds

I still wasn't sure how I was feeling about Kendall and Molly and the whole of the Booth crowd since our weekend away.

As good as it had felt to have those private chats with Kendall, and to hear how she thought I was special to her, I wasn't sure I truly liked the rest of them very much. I knew that didn't necessarily matter, and getting in with them was all part of a bigger plan to expand my social circle, but I still felt like it might be good to have some space from them, so I deliberately stayed out of their way for a few days, spending Monday and Tuesday going to my lessons, focusing on my work and trying to get into the pre-holiday Christmas spirit.

But on Wednesday lunchtime, I got a message from Kendall.

EMERGENCY!
Last-minute booking! Could be good!
Bashed meeting at mine tonight. 7 p.m.

When I arrived in Kendall's room that evening, Molly was in her usual position looking at her phone on Kendall's bed.

'Oh, good you're here,' Kendall said, 'Sit down, sit down. We need to get straight on with things. We've had a request. It's kind of short notice and it's kind of intense but it could be big for Bashed.'

I took a seat on the end of the bed. 'What is it?'

Kendall spun her chair round so she was looking right at me. 'OK, so you know Pamela? Pamela Roach? The one who loved your bingo? It's for her. The request is from her.'

Kendall explained that the venue that Pamela had arranged months ago to hold her work Christmas party had flooded and had to pull out, so she was on a frantic search for a last-minute replacement.

'It was going to be a masked ball. For, like, fifty people! So that's what she still wants. She's found a new venue – some hotel on the seafront – but we have to do the food and the cake. That's OK but here's the crucial bit: she wants us to provide the masks.'

'The masks?' I said. 'Don't people normally bring their own to a masked ball?'

It wasn't the type of event I'd ever been called to attend myself, but Mum and Dad had been to a masked ball once for Dad's work and had been very proud of the Venetian masks they'd ordered from actual, real Venice especially for the occasion.

Kendall shook her head. 'She wants it to be a surprise. So no one even knows it's going to be a masked ball until they show up and Pamela is like, "Surprise! Wear a mask!"'

'Right,' I said. 'OK.'

'So, the point is,' Kendall went on, 'we have to source fifty masks by Saturday. But it's OK because I found this website where you can order them bespoke.' She flipped open her laptop to show me. 'You see? You just put in colour, style, decoration, et cetera, then they put them all together and send them to you. And we've got budget, Gracie. Pamela's given us eight hundred big ones to get the whole thing sorted.'

'Eight hundred pounds?' This seemed a massive amount of money.

Kendall nodded. 'I know. Mad, isn't it.'

I peered at the website on Kendall's screen. It was open on a website called New Faces, on a page called 'How it works'.

It explained how you could use the site to create and order your bespoke masks, and listed the prices, the lowest of which was ten pounds, for the most basic mask design.

'Ten pounds each,' I said. 'So . . . five hundred pounds, for the fifty?'

Kendall nodded. 'Yep. We'd need a hundred to pay for the food and stuff, so that's then twenty or so to pay for the cake stuff. So that's a sweet two hundred left over for us.'

I thought of Mac, probably sitting as we spoke on a bed in his B & B room, looking at his cactus with the ribbon tied around it, no idea what his Christmas was going to be like or how he might start rebuilding his life afterwards.

'So that's two hundred we could give to Mac then,' I said. 'Isn't it?'

Kendall turned around, surprised. Then she crinkled her nose. 'Well, not really, Gracie. I mean, that's our salary, you know? Me and Mol have to put in a lot of work to do all that food. We can't work for free. That's basically illegal.

And there's you too – you're in charge of designing the masks on that website and ordering them. Which I know isn't as big a deal as making an enormous buffet like we have to but will still take time.'

'Oh, I don't mind working for free,' I said. 'I don't mind giving my salary to Mac.'

Kendall raised her eyebrows. 'Fair enough, Mother Teresa,' she said. 'Call it twenty quid then. He's welcome to that.'

Twenty pounds? Was that really all we could spare from a massive cheque of eight hundred?

The truth was, I didn't understand much about how Kendall did the accounts for each party. I knew that all the money came to her, and that I got my small fee plus any cash I needed for specific purchases, like when I'd had to buy the Santa presents, but what she did with the rest was a mystery. All I knew was that so far, we hadn't managed to give anything at all to Mac, even though we had a big banner on our website that said we were going to.

'What if,' I said carefully, 'I didn't spend five hundred on the masks? Could I give anything spare from that to him?'

'That's the cheapest site,' Molly said, chipping in for the first time. 'The cheapest masks on the cheapest site are a tenner. You won't find individual masks cheaper than that.'

'And,' Kendall added, 'Pamela was very clear that they all have to be different. We can't just buy a job lot of fifty matching ones.'

'OK, so what about if I made them?' I said. 'I reckon I can do fifty masks for way cheaper than five hundred pounds.'

Kendall raised an eyebrow. '*Fifty*, Gracie?'

I nodded. 'Yeah! I'm sure I can do it. Easy. Well, maybe not easy, but definitely possible. So how about, you give me the five hundred pounds for the masks as planned and it's up to me how I make them. Anything I can save by doing it myself, I can donate to Mac.'

Kendall looked at me. 'What *is* it about you and the caretaker?'

'Nothing,' I said. 'I just feel sorry for him.'

Kendall sighed. 'I always tell you, Gracie: you're too nice.'

I shrugged. 'So I can do it my way?'

'Sure. If that's what you really want.'

And I was almost surprised that I really, really did. Not to make Mac or anyone else like me. Not to impress Kendall.

Just because it seemed like the right thing to do.

My Own Project

With Christmas six days away and college finished for the
year, I should have been enjoying the run-up as I normally
would. One small benefit of having a very little brother is
that Christmas gets some of the magic back that you forget
about when you're not a little kid yourself.

On Thursday morning, the first day of my Christmas
holiday, I went downstairs to find Ollie helping Paddy make
a stocking out of some of the red felt and white fur left over
from the Santa outfit I'd had to make and wear myself for
Marie's Father Christmas party a week earlier, where I'd
handed out the presents I'd carefully selected and generally
shown everyone a good time.

It looked like it was Ollie who was doing the actual
making of the stocking because Paddy was drawing intently
in a blank exercise book.

'What are you working on, Padster?' I said, stroking his
hair.

'Stories for Santa,' he said without looking up.

'Why?' I said.

'It's about a snake who swims to the bottom of the sea to buy a hamburger,' he said, which in no way answered my question.

'His theory is,' Ollie said, carefully running a line of PVA glue down the edge of the stocking, 'that if he leaves a book of great adventure stories out for Father Christmas, the old guy will sit down and have a read . . . and the longer he stays, the more presents he will get? Something like that, anyway.'

'Right,' I said. 'A flawless plan.'

Paddy held out his pencil to me. 'Please will you draw me a hamburger, Gracie?'

'I can't stop, I'm afraid,' I said to him. 'Ollie will help you. I've got my own project to get on with.'

And although I would really have liked to sit down in the warm kitchen with Ollie and Paddy and worked idly on Paddy's projects while the radio played Christmas songs in the background, I knew that with three days to make fifty masks, I didn't have time to be idly doing anything. These were fifty masks that someone had paid several hundreds of pounds for, so I couldn't just cut a paper plate in half and cover it with glitter. These had to be smart, neat, professional.

Last night, after several hours searching the internet for advice and tutorials on mask-making, I'd worked out how I was going to do it.

I'd discovered that in an ideal world, the best way to craft a high-end Venetian mask involved buying a silicon model of a face, applying papier mâché to it to create the shape of the mask and decorating the shell when it was dry. The only problem was, as I had to make all fifty masks at the

208

same time, I would need to buy fifty silicon moulds to get them all done. And silicon moulds didn't come cheap, so that would basically wipe out my entire budget before I'd even begun, meaning it would be cheaper to order them from the website Kendall wanted to use in the first place.

However, after staying up past midnight experimenting with an entire roll of tin foil in my bedroom, I realised that if I layered several pieces together to make a thick metal sheet, I could bend it into the approximate shape of a face and use this as my mould instead. So, the first part of my task was to buy ten boxes of foil, and spend today fashioning them into fifty silver faces.

By mid-morning, I was in my room surrounded by the foil. As I'd discovered the night before, by far the quickest way to mould foil into the shape of a face was to push the layer of metal against my own face, smoothing the foil around my nose and eyes to create the contours. Once I'd done that I had a realistic, if slightly fragile, metal base to work from.

I can't lie; the job was hard.

It was OK to begin with, but it turned out that fifty was a lot of times to smother your face with a foil sheet and, as I got into the early thirties, each one was coming away shiny with sweat. I wondered if the people who did glamourous things like go to masked balls realised the toil that went on in the background to create their props.

By four o'clock, two hours ahead of schedule, I had fifty metal faces lined up across my bedroom floor, staring up at me like a spooky alien choir. It was time to move onto the next stage – tearing newspaper into pieces, soaking it in a mixture of flour and water, and draping the strips over the metal. All the time I was doing it, I tried to keep in mind the high fee the customer was paying and take special care to make sure the job was neat and professional. This wasn't like when I'd made Paddy a zebra costume out of my old pyjamas and a pair of tights for zoo day at nursery. These had to be absolutely perfect.

By eleven o'clock, all fifty moulds were covered with sodden newspaper and glue and there was nothing for me to do but climb into bed in the middle of the sea of blank faces staring up at the ceiling and wait for them to dry.

The next morning, the papier mâché was drier than when I'd applied it but still wasn't dry enough for me to be able to peel it from the foil. I stood in the middle of the room surveying the scene. I had known this was a risk. It was the middle of winter and damp outside; I'd known drying time would be compromised. There wasn't room to put even three or four in the airing cupboard, so I needed to think of something else.

I realised there was nothing for it but to manually dry each one, so I spent the next hour on my hands and knees crawling amongst the faces, blasting each of them in turn with the hairdryer.

By lunchtime they were dry. Or dry enough – time was of the essence and I couldn't wait any longer. I picked up the crispest of the batch and peeled the paper shell away from the foil face. There was one nerve-wracking moment where the forehead began to crack, but in the end it came away cleanly.

'Yes!' I said out loud to no one, holding the mask above my head in celebration.

It took another two hours to peel the rest of them away, and then another hour to cover my carpet with newspaper, open all the windows and spray them with bright white paint. By this time, it was ten o'clock and, worn out from another full day's mask making, I went to bed.

The next day was Saturday and I had just nine hours to get the masks finished and delivered to Pamela's party on the sea-front.

Mum, Dad, Ollie and Paddy had all gone to London for the day to see the Christmas lights and some carols and other things that I would really have liked to be doing myself, but I had to stay focused. Any time I felt a pang of sadness about missing out on my family Christmas, I thought of Mac and Mrs Mac, sitting on their bed in their B & B, looking at their small Christmas cactus.

All that was left for me to do was decorate the masks with the black, gold and silver permanent markers I'd bought for the purpose. Now I was approaching the final stage of the project, I was almost enjoying myself, carefully drawing circles around the eyes and adding flamboyant swirls to the foreheads and cheeks, each one of them different.

As I set down the last finished mask, I looked at my watch. It was three o'clock and I was exhausted. Kendall was due to pick me up at four to collect the masks and deliver them to the party, so I had an hour to rest before I had to load them into a box and head out.

The next thing I knew, my phone was buzzing on my pillow next to my head. I woke up with a start and tilted the screen towards me. The first thing I noticed was Kendall's name on the screen, alongside fourteen missed calls. The second thing I noticed was that the clock next to my bed said five thirty. I sat up suddenly and scrambled to answer the phone.

'Kendall, I'm so sorry! I fell asleep'.

'Grace, Jesus, where are you? I'm outside your house. We need the masks NOW or we can say goodbye to our eight hundred quid. And to ever getting any business from anyone at that party again!'

'I'm coming, I'm coming, give me five minutes to box them up.'

I loaded the fifty masks into four cardboard boxes, stacking them all carefully to make sure they didn't get bent or damaged. They looked good but I knew the way I'd made them meant they were for temporary enjoyment only. They wouldn't survive a drink being spilt on them or getting caught in the rain or any rough handling at all. All I hoped was by the time they did start to look a bit worn around the edges, the party would be in full swing and no one would notice.

I piled the boxes on top of each other and made my way down the stairs, feeling with my feet for each step. I opened the front door and squinted out into the street, looking for Kendall's blue car. But there were no cars parked outside the house at all.

'There you are! Basically gave me a heart attack, Grace!'

Kendall stepped into the drive from behind the wall. She was holding onto the handle bars of the bike I had used to deliver Pamela Roach's birthday cake and buffet, complete with rickety metal trailer on the back.

I frowned. 'Where's your car?'

'That's the thing, isn't it – it's not my car! It's my sister's, I just use it when she's at uni. But right now she's back and she wanted it tonight. If you'd come out at four like we arranged it would have been OK but now I've had to give it back to her!'

I groaned. 'Oh god, I'm sorry. I've just been so tired, it's taken so many hours to make this lot.' The boxes swayed unsteadily in my arms. 'But it will be fine. I can take them in the trailer, no problem. I've ridden the bike before. It will be fine.'

'OK, but you need to get going. They need to be there in half an hour.'

I nodded and began to load the boxes into the trailer. 'Will I meet you there? Where's the cake? And the food?'

Kendall shook her head. 'I already took all that earlier. And I need to go now. Eddie's back in town.'

'Eddie? Ex-Eddie?' I felt the slightest pang of jealousy at the thought of Kendall on her romantic date with this boy she was obsessed with, even though from what I'd heard there seemed to be nothing very much to like about him at all.

She nodded, suddenly unable to meet my eye. 'Yeah. He wants to go for dinner to talk, so I can listen to what he has to say at least. I'm not saying I'm going to do anything about it.'

'Right,' I nodded. 'OK. That's fine. All fine. You get off then. I'll be fine from here.'

As I climbed onto the bike and made my way out into the road, I wondered how many times you had to say the word 'fine' for it to be true.

I pedalled slowly, trying to second-guess the direction the trailer would swing, and at the same time making sure I didn't hit any kerbs or bumps in the road that would upset my delicate cargo. Late afternoon in late December is a very dark time on the streets and the feeble light on the front of my bike only really lit a few feet in front of me. Every time I heard a car approach, I pulled over entirely and waited for it to pass, so nervous was I that the trailer might make a sudden lurch into its path, pulling the bike, the masks and me with it.

After twenty minutes of careful weaving around the roads, I was still a good distance from the hotel. I took out my phone and consulted the map and as I did so, I realised I could take a short cut across the park. This would not only save me time, but would hopefully be less scary as I wouldn't have to worry about cars.

I got off the bike to wheel it through the narrow gate and close it behind me, then I had a clear run of several hundred metres through the park where I could hopefully make up some time.

As I was trundling along, the metal box clattering behind me, I heard a dog bark. I tried to look, but any turning of my head made me swerve dangerously so I kept facing forward and ignored whatever the dog was doing. But the barking was getting louder and added to it was the sound of paw on concrete and I realised then that the dog was chasing me, no doubt excited by the bouncing trailer full of disembodied faces I was pulling behind me.

I slowed just enough to let me to turn to look at exactly what was going on, and at the same moment I realised who the dog was, I heard a shout:

'Lady Gaga! No! Come here!'

It wasn't Til though, calling the dog's name, nor her mum. It was a man's voice. As he got nearer I noticed he had a long beard, like a wizard. I realised this must be Malcolm, the man Til, her mum and Lady Gaga were currently living with.

'No, Lady Gaga!' I shouted, continuing to pedal forward. Under normal circumstances I would have stopped to stroke her and reassure her everything was OK but I had to protect my shipment. 'Get away! Leave!'

All I could do was to try and outpace her – surely I could move faster on a wheeled vehicle than a dog could move on its legs alone, even an enormous animal like Lady Gaga? – and I was now zooming along the outside of the lake at speed. But Lady Gaga just would not tire, and if anything, she was getting closer. I took one hand off the handle bars and made a wild flapping motion with my arm to shoo her away, and as I did so, my wheel hit a dip in the path, not so much a puddle as a mud slick.

My front wheel skidded to the side and the whole bike, the trailer, the masks and me toppled sideways into the lake.

A Total Disaster

I screamed as the ice-cold water flooded inside my clothes. My legs were tangled up with the bike.

'Help!' I screamed, getting a mouthful of muddy water.

Although we always called the lake in the park 'the lake' it was really more of a pond. It was probably no more than two feet deep and was made up partly of water, partly of something the consistency and colour of treacle. The whole thing smelt like a very badly kept cow shed.

As I tried to pull myself out from under the bike, the pain hit me. A sharp, shooting pain right across my chest and down my arm.

'Ow!' I shouted. 'OW!'

The trailer had flipped onto its side and the masks had spilled out into the water. Already some were floating off across the surface like big white lily pads.

'The masks!' I shouted, making a lunge for them, but the pain in my shoulder shot through me again and I was forced to stop.

And then Lady Gaga jumped in to join me. Clearly

delighted at the sight of my beautiful masks roaming free across the lake, she threw herself into the water and began a splashy half-run, half-swim in pursuit of them, her tail flapping about wildly as she changed direction, unable to decide which of the masks to go after first.

'No!' I shouted. 'Leave!' But she didn't even pause, and anyway, I knew it was pointless. I knew that the masks were already ruined. Even a light dusting of rain would have been enough to wreck the paintwork and bend the papier mâché shells out of shape. A full submersion in a muddy pond would be sure to turn them into porridge.

'Lady!' Malcolm shouted. 'Lady Gaga, come here!'

He was standing on the edge of the pond now across the water from me, wearing a red anorak and a blue hat, his beard tossed over his left shoulder.

'Help!' I shouted to him. 'Can you help me?'

He peered towards me. 'Hello?' he shouted. 'I can't see you? Where are you?'

'In the lake!' I shouted back.

'Oh, good gracious,' he said, and started to jog towards me.

Lady Gaga meanwhile had caught up with one of the masks and seized it in her mouth. What had once been a crisp papier mâché shell was now a pliable sticky mess, and, as Lady Gaga frolicked happily about the pond holding it in her mouth, the mask folded backwards and perfectly covered her face, giving the unsettling impression that there was a giant Newfoundland dog in the middle of the park lake wearing a Venetian mask and dancing.

I realised I had no choice but to leave her to it. The masks were lost. I needed to concentrate on getting out of the water and addressing whatever this incredible pain in my shoulder was.

'Are you OK?' Malcolm said as he approached.

'No!' was all I could manage to wail back.

'Here, grab on,' he said, holding out his hand. I tried to reach out but the pain made me pull away at the last minute and he stumbled forward, landing next to me in the water. Lady Gaga, delighted that someone else had come in to join the party, sprinted over still wearing the mask and began splashing us both enthusiastically.

'It's freezing!' Malcolm shouted. 'Get off, Lady Gaga! What is that? What have you got?'

'It's a Venetian mask,' I explained unhappily.

Suddenly I felt my chest was vibrating and I remembered I'd tucked my phone into the inside pocket of my jacket to protect it for the bike ride. This I realised was a stroke of luck as it had probably saved it from the worst of the water.

I answered it. 'Hello?'

'Grace, where the hell are you? Pamela's called me, saying you were supposed to be there fifteen minutes ago!'

'Kendall! I'm in a lake!'

'What?'

'I fell in! In Queen's Park! Til's dog chased me and now the dog is wearing a mask and I'm stuck in the water!'

Suddenly my phone cut out. I didn't know if Kendall had hung up on me or if my battery was flat or if the phone was broken from the water after all. I tucked it back into my coat, and with one big movement made myself ignore the pain and push the bike off me. Using my one good arm, I pushed myself to my feet so the water was now only mid-thigh deep.

Malcolm had managed to get himself upright too and he guided me out of the water and onto the bank.

We both sat on the floor, breathing hard. I began to shiver wildly, my whole body shaking. The bike was still in the water, lying sadly on its side. The whole surface of the lake was now covered with drifting, disintegrating paper masks, and Lady Gaga was wandering between them, sniffing at some, batting a paw at others, like a visitor to a rose garden.

'Grace!' I looked towards the shout and saw Kendall coming through the park gates. She was running towards me but she was wearing heels so high that it looked like she was wearing someone else's legs and she hadn't yet worked out how to use them.

'What are you doing?' She looked at Malcolm. 'What have you done to her?'

'Nothing!' he protested. 'She fell in!'

Kendall looked at my bike, sticking up at a strange angle, its back wheel in the air. She squinted out across the water, trying to make sense of the white shapes covering the surface.

'Oh no,' she said, shaking her head. 'Oh *no*.' Then she turned to look at me, aghast. 'Grace? Not the masks?'

I nodded sadly. 'The dog chased me. Lady Gaga. It wasn't my fault.'

Kendall shook her head slowly, then she ran her hand through her hair. 'Jesus, Grace! They've paid for them!'

'We'll give the money back . . .' I said quietly.

'I was just ten minutes ago telling Eddie how we'd absolutely nailed our biggest gig yet but now here you are, being a total disaster!'

'I know,' I said quietly. 'I know.'

Malcolm climbed to his feet. 'I need to get Lady Gaga home. And I need to get out of these wet things. You should do the same. Hypothermia can set in really quickly, you know.' He looked up at Kendall. 'Get her home and dry.'

Malcolm whistled and finally Lady Gaga seemed to tire of the masks and bounded over to him and the two of them left the park.

'Lady Gaga chased me,' I told Kendall again.

She sighed and then she said, 'Only you, Grace. Could only happen to you.'

I wasn't sure that was true. Lady Gaga would have quite happily followed anyone who happened to be cycling along with a metal box full of masks behind them, but I decided now wasn't the time to argue this point.

Kendall sighed again, but then a small smile appeared at the edge of her mouth. She shook her head and laughed. Then she said, 'Jesus!' again and much to my surprise, pulled out her phone and took a series of quickfire photos – the bike in the water, the masks drifting outwards from the trailer like an oil slick, then me half sitting, half lying on the ground.

'What are you doing?' I said, still struggling to talk through my chattering teeth.

'We'll look back and laugh one day.' She put her phone away and said, 'Come on then,' and tried to pull me up.

'Ow!' I screamed, trying to put my hand on the source of the pain, but not being totally sure where it was. 'Don't!'

Kendall stepped away. 'I barely touched you.'

'I've hurt my arm,' I said. 'I think maybe . . . maybe we should call an ambulance.'

Kendall smiled, her head on one side. 'Gracie, are you sure you're not being a bit dramatic?'

'I think –'

But I don't know what I was going to say I was thinking, or if it was from the cold or the pain or shock, or from all three combined with the exhaustion of the seventy-two-hour mask-making program, but whatever it was it made me faint, right there in the middle of the park.

Hospital

When I next opened my eyes, I was still in the dark park but there were people and noises all around me.

I was lying flat on my back now with a circle of faces above me and I'd been wrapped in a foil sheet. I felt like a baked potato that had been got all ready to go into the oven and for some reason this was the thought my mind decided to deliver to my mouth and when I opened my mouth to ask what was going on the only word that came out was 'potato'.

'We'll get you something to eat in a bit, love,' said an ambulance woman in a green suit. 'Let's just get you checked out first.'

She and the man with her tried to lift me to my feet. They were slower and gentler than Kendall had been but still I winced and shrank away from them.

'That sore, is it?' the woman said.

'Yeah,' I said, my voice coming out as a whisper.

'You might have broken your collar-bone,' she said. 'If we can get you up we can get you to the hospital to get you checked out.'

I suppose I must have looked nervous at the mention of the hospital because she said, 'Don't worry, your friend can come along too,' and Kendall smiled around at everyone.

Once we were in the ambulance, me strapped to a chair still in my baked potato outfit, the ambulance lady asked exactly how I'd come to be soaking wet and passed out next to the lake and Kendall seemed happy to explain, which I was relieved about because I was too exhausted to talk.

'So basically, what happened,' Kendall said, 'is that Grace was cycling with a delivery to our customers – a delivery of masks. We have this business, you see – we founded it. Grace is an employee, but it's my business. Anyway, she was cycling a delivery on a company bike and this mad wild dog got loose and started chasing her and jumped up at her bike and pushed her into the lake. And she got stuck under the bike so she was basically drowning, and the wild dog was still there, literally trying to eat her, and the dog's owner was absolutely no help. So I had to like, wade in and wrestle the dog off and pull her to the side of the lake. And I was going to give her mouth-to-mouth and everything but luckily she started breathing just in time.'

The ambulance woman smiled kindly. 'I see,' she said in the same voice you might use on a three-year-old who told you they'd visited Jupiter in their summer holiday. 'Well, it all sounds very frightening.'

When we got to the hospital and the ambulance people handed me over to some other doctors and nurses, Kendall once again was able to recount the story of her epic rescue.

I didn't even care at this point. I was just relieved that once she'd realised I was actually hurt she'd stopped seeming so annoyed about the lost masks. All I wanted now was to be warm and dry and for the pain to go away.

And I wanted my mum.

Mum

The doctors cut off my clothes and gave me a strange crispy hospital gown to wear. As Kendall hovered at the side of my wheelie bed she eyed my blotchy, semi-hairy legs with interest. 'I think it's very brave, the way you don't care about shaving your legs.'

I didn't say anything. I was glad the blue wax was all gone, at least.

'In fact,' she went on, 'you never really care what you look like at all, do you?' She looked at me in fascination. 'It's so . . . *brave*.'

A doctor gave me an injection to help with the pain, meaning the next hour passed by in a confused fog, but by the time Mum had been contacted, and managed to get the train down from London and a taxi to the hospital, I had been X-rayed and it had been confirmed that I did indeed have a broken collar-bone.

'Oh, Grace!' Mum said, rushing into the cubicle. 'What have you been doing? What were you even doing on a bike?'

'I had to take the masks . . .' I started, but my voice was slurring and I couldn't put the story together.

'It was the masks,' Kendall cut in. 'Really, it was a turning point in the Bashed journey, an event this prestigious, so we all had to go the extra mile to deliver for our customers.'

'I see,' Mum said, not taking her eyes off me.

'I'm Kendall, by the way,' Kendall told Mum, holding out her hand. 'The Managing Director of Bashed Events Limited.'

Mum looked at Kendall for the first time then, a slight frown on her face. 'You're Kendall, are you. I see.' She took Kendall's hand and shook it for only the briefest of moments.

'I've called the customer and told them what's happened,' Kendall went on. 'And obviously she was disappointed to have her whole party ruined literally ten minutes before it started.'

'Yes,' said Mum tightly.

'But I've explained that these things happen.' Kendall turned to me now. 'And she was very worried and hopes you're OK. I told her you were and that you'd find a way to make it up to her.'

I couldn't think of any possible way I could do that. The idea of making another fifty masks and cycling them through a dark park made me want to go to sleep for a very long time.

We were waiting for the doctor to come and talk to us and tell us what would be happening next. 'Have you had a hot drink, Grace?' Mum said. 'I'll get you one. You need something hot.'

Mum left in search of a drinks machine and Kendall took the opportunity to lean in to me and say, 'Don't worry, I'm great at handling mums,' like mums were giant hairy spiders

226

that needed to be caught and disposed of.

'What happened with Eddie?' I asked. 'Your date?'

'Oh that . . .' She looked out of the window. 'Turns out he just wanted to tell me he's seeing someone now – some twenty-year-old grandma! – so he's not going to be in touch as much.'

'Oh,' I said quietly. 'I'm sorry.'

'Oh, I literally could not care less,' Kendall said, her voice breezy again. 'And I told him as much. And I told him how well Bashed was going without him and he had to admit everything down here is much better for me now he's gone.'

I nodded. 'OK,' I said. 'Good.'

Mum came back with a steaming paper cup and she helped me lean forward in my bed to get closer to it. Then the doctor returned.

'So yes,' he said. 'As I think you've already been told the clavicle is fractured, so –'

'Will she get a plaster cast?' Kendall said. 'We could all sign it! And, oh my god, Grace, you know what we could do? We could draw the Bashed logo on it and post the pictures online which would be a great way to –'

But the doctor was shaking his head. 'No plaster cast for broken collar-bones. Just this sling to immobilise the arm while it heals.'

'Oh,' Kendall said, disappointed.

'It is a moderately severe break though,' the doctor went on once he'd finished manoeuvring me into the sling, 'so we'll monitor it, but there is a chance you might need surgery to realign the bones.'

'Surgery!' said Kendall and Mum at the same time.

The doctor nodded. 'Potentially. But let's see how we go. Either way, you will make a full recovery. Just avoid dogs and lakes and bikes – at least avoid all three at the same time!'

I gave the doctor a tired smile and Mum thanked him and then put her hand on my forehead and said, 'Let's get you home to your bed then.'

'I'll give you a call about the plan for making it up to Pamela,' Kendall said as Mum eased me off the bed.

'Grace is on sick leave for the time being, Kendall,' Mum said in a tone that surprised me and, by the look on her face, Kendall.

But when Mum talks like that, it's not worth arguing.

I didn't say anything, and Kendall nodded and said, 'Sure,' quietly.

When I got home and Mum had helped me into some pyjamas, I ask her to get my phone that was still in the inside pocket of my coat. Once I'd plugged it in and let it charge for a few minutes it booted itself up as normal, seemingly suffering no ill effects from our adventure. In fact, I saw I had loads of notifications.

I realised they were all coming from a photo Kendall had put up that she had tagged me in. I scrolled through the three photos that made up the post: the masks drifting across the lake, the bike stuck in the mud and me, hair pasted across the side of my face and mud smeared across my lip like an extravagant moustache, my mouth hanging open like a dopey drunk.

I read the caption:

What a day! Grace managed to cycle into a swamp and nearly died! Luckily I was able to get her out in time! #doanythingformymates #DIYhero

I read the comments underneath the post which were a mixture of 'ouch' and 'fail!' and people congratulating Kendall. 'Well done, K. I can't think of anyone better in a crisis,' someone said.

By the time I'd read all the messages, I was left feeling like I was a silly clumsy child who had ridden into a swamp on purpose and that Kendall had had to put her own life on the line to rescue me.

I sighed and leant back carefully on my pillow. I supposed that was just the way it went with stories like these. By the time they spread around they took on a life of their own. And in a way, it was exciting to be the centre of attention.

The more I thought about it, the more this was proof of how far I had come. A few weeks ago no one would have cared if I'd fallen off my bike. Maybe Til and Reeta would have messaged me. If that. But now hundreds of people had seen Kendall's post. People were commenting on it; people knew who I was. People cared.

I decided that the best way to take something good from an unfortunate situation was to capitalise on it. And the best way to do that was to go along with the story people wanted to hear.

I took a photo of myself lying in bed, my sling on display.

I carefully set my face into an expression that said 'comically glum' rather than revealed how tired and sore and fed up I actually was – people want a fun sob story not a whiney sob story – then I uploaded it with the caption:

Broken collar-bone, got to have surgery but so lucky that Kendall was there to rescue me! #friendship #grateful

After posting it I fell asleep but the next morning I woke up and saw that the photo had turned out to be one of the most popular posts I'd ever made.

Christmas Invalid

With the first few days of the Christmas holiday spent hiding in my room making fifty foil faces followed by fifty black-and-white masks, and then the week of Christmas itself spent trying to hold my whole body as still as possible to avoid disrupting my cracked bones, and with Mum and Dad dispensing regular doses of painkillers that made me feel like I was watching everything around me through a slightly dirty plastic screen, I felt like I virtually missed out on Christmas altogether.

When Paddy was excitedly running around shouting about his presents, Mum had to keep warning him to stay away from my chair, which was already positioned a safe distance away from the main action at the end of the room. I felt too sick from the painkillers and too tired from not being able to sleep properly to eat any of the masses of food my parents had stockpiled.

Usually my favourite part of Christmas is giving the presents, not because I am some kind of super-generous saint, but because I am actually really good at choosing presents and usually so organised that I sometimes have everyone's presents sorted by October. But this year I'd been so busy with my popularity field notes and then Bashed and then thinking about Kendall that I'd just bought the first vaguely acceptable thing I could find on the internet, so although there was nothing particularly wrong with the socks I gave Dad or the bath oil I gave Mum or the yard of Jaffa Cakes I got Ollie, I knew those presents could have been bought by any stranger on the street.

By the day before New Year's Eve, I had barely left the house in nine days and I was sick of switching between watching TV on the sofa and watching TV in bed. I was bored and miserable.

At one point, Mum commented, 'Maybe now you've experienced an injury you might have a bit of sympathy for me when my back goes?'

Although I didn't really think it was a good thing for a mother to be smug about their daughter's bad luck, I did feel bad about the times I made a fuss about the favours Mum had asked of me when she was laid up, seeing as now it was the other way around and I couldn't so much as open a jar of Marmite without having to call her to help.

'I *did* have sympathy,' I protested. 'I just . . .' I wasn't sure what my point was going to be so I trailed off. 'Fine,' I said in the end. 'I'm sorry I'm always so annoying.'

Mum just smiled and kissed me on the forehead. 'Not *always*, love.'

Normally New Year's Eve is a complete non-event for me. At an absolute stretch, Til may come around to watch a

232

film and we might put the fireworks on the TV at midnight, but usually I just sleep right through the whole thing. This year however, I was excited to see I'd been invited to a party hosted by Booth member Josh, with the locker next to mine. Obviously my efforts at conversation while we unloaded our books hadn't gone unnoticed.

He didn't invite me himself; Molly sent a message to the Bashed message group asking if I was going, but before I could reply, Kendall jumped in:

Kendall: Of course she can't come, Mol! She's broken her neck! She's waiting for surgery!

And I realised I was relieved, really. I wanted to be invited to things, sure, but that didn't mean I necessarily wanted to go to them.

Kendall, Molly and all the others kept in constant contact with me over that week, which was nice. This mostly took the form of long messages or videos of themselves talking to each other and blowing me kisses. 'Miss you!' they always said at the end.

'You can come over if you like,' I replied once, feeling a bit nervous about having them in my actual house and wondering if I should tidy or put out some quirky ornaments or something, but it didn't matter because there was always something else they had to be doing and by the time we'd fixed a time when it might happen, I figured it would be easier to just see them when we were back at college.

Someone who didn't bother with making plans and waiting

for an invite was Til, who arrived in my bedroom on New Year's Day.

'All right,' she said, strolling in and going to look out the window, like she always did when she arrived in a new place, as if she was making sure we weren't being spied on.

'I've been better but I'm OK,' I said bravely.

'Lady Gaga is sorry, you know,' she said. 'I mean, she hasn't exactly said so, but she probably is. She's not mean.'

'I know,' I said. 'It's OK.'

'And Malcolm is too, for not controlling her. But she can be a handful so . . .'

'It's OK,' I said again. 'She was just excited.'

Til nodded. 'Brought you this.' She took an apple out of her jacket pocket and put it on my bedside table.

I looked at it. 'Why?'

'That's what you give to the sick, isn't it? Apples?'

I frowned. 'I think that's teachers. And ponies.'

She thought about this, then shrugged. 'Oh well.'

She sat on my bed and I winced to show her how much pain I was in, but she didn't notice.

'What have you been doing?' she said.

'Not a lot.'

She nodded again. She was never exactly chatty but she was being quiet even for her.

'What's the matter?' I said.

I expected her to say 'Nothing' like she always did and then we could go back to sitting there in silence until we both just got our phones out and looked at those instead, but much to my surprise she said:

234

'It's the flat thing. Living with Malcolm is awful. My bedroom is a conservatory. Not even a conservatory, because that sounds big. This room is so small I have to fold my bed up every morning. And it's where the front door is so when he comes home late he has to walk right over me. I'm getting no sleep and I've got nowhere to leave my stuff.'

'It's only temporary though, isn't it?'

Til shrugged. 'It's meant to be. But where else is there? Even if I can persuade Mum to rehome Lady Gaga it's still not easy to find places.'

I nodded. It did sound difficult, but I didn't know what I could do. I also honestly believed that it would be OK, one way or another, in the end. People didn't just get thrown onto the streets. She wasn't going to have to move all her furniture into the middle of the road and sit there under the stars. You just didn't see it.

It wasn't that I didn't care, I suppose I just thought we'd got to the end of that part of the conversation. She'd outlined her concerns, I'd responded empathetically, so I thought it was OK to move on.

'My surgery is going to be on Friday,' I said. 'Then I should be back at college the week after.'

Til nodded again. She walked around my room, picking things up and putting them down again, but it felt like neither of us had anything to say to each other.

In the end, she said she had to get going and she left.

Later that day, I went down to Podrick's. I had already explained on the phone to Leonard that I wouldn't be able to come to work for six weeks and, to be fair, he hadn't said 'That's annoying for me' or 'Who am I supposed to get to cover you?'. He just said he hoped I got better soon but he sounded kind of weary about the whole business. And so partly because I wanted to show him I was genuinely injured, and partly because I needed to get out of the house, I went down to the shop in person.

Sheila was sitting behind the counter reading her magazine.

'Look at you,' she said, looking me up and down. 'Came a cropper, I heard.'

'Yeah,' I said.

'Back to college soon?'

'Yeah.'

She turned a page of her magazine. 'Well,' she said slowly. 'You want some advice?'

'OK,' I said, even though I didn't.

'Watch out for storm chasers.'

'Huh?' I said. 'Those people who chase hurricanes in America?'

She shook her head. 'No. Not that. You heard of fair-weather friends, haven't you? People who are only there when the going is good? It's like that, but these are people who are only there when times are stormy. Leeches for drama. I can't bear them.'

'OK,' I agreed, but I had no idea what she was on about.

Back to College

I got the bad news on the 2nd January:

I didn't need surgery.

I went with Dad to the hospital and as the doctor examined my X-rays, he said, 'Yes, good. All seems to be healing nicely on its own. So we can avoid surgical intervention altogether.'

'But I've told everyone I'm having surgery,' I said.

Dad raised his eyebrows. 'I'm sure they'll get over the disappointment.'

I still had my sling, which the doctor said I would probably have to wear for a few more weeks, but I felt flat. I thought we'd been gearing up to more drama but now that was it. No more excitement, just boredom and discomfort.

'That's good then,' Ollie said when Dad and I returned home and told him the news. 'Isn't it? Why do you look so miserable?'

'I think Grace was hoping to enjoy ill-health for a little bit longer,' Dad said in that loud whisper he always does when he's making fun of me when I'm right there.

'I just think,' I said indignantly, 'that they shouldn't tell you they're going to provide you with a service and then not bother! It makes you look silly when you have told a lot of people about that service!'

Ollie rolled his eyes. 'This girl on my course has to have surgery to replace a whole kidney so you can't be moaning because you don't have to have surgery when she would love to not be having surgery.'

'Don't really see what that's got to do with anything but fine.' I turned away from him and used my good arm to fill the kettle.

'Are you going to go back to college then?' Dad said.

'Tomorrow,' I said.

And I did go back, because although I could have enjoyed a few more rehab days at home with no one in the house and a cupboard full of food at my disposal, I had enjoyed all the messages of support I'd got from everyone and I was ready to soak up the real-life version.

The first hour of my return to college was fun.

I knew that, in a way, Sheila was right and some of the people fussing around me and asking to see my bruises were just storm chasers, interested in anything as long as there was a bit of drama – but in the end I thought, who cares? Why does it matter why people are interested in me? Back in November, when no one had been interested in me at all, I would have tried anything. I did try anything: new clothes, new activities. The important thing, I knew, was that they would talk to me, and I would talk back and that's how they would realise I was cool. I just needed the hook. And if the hook was a sling and a broken collar-bone, then so be it.

When Kendall called from the Booth, 'Looks who it is! Back from the dead!', I played my part with enthusiasm, pushing my bottom lip out in a pout and doing an exaggerated comedy walk as if I had a broken ankle as well as broken collar-bone. When people shuffled up and I was allowed a seat in the Booth – which despite all our work together in Bashed, I had never been offered before – and Kendall once again told the story of how she'd waded in to rescue me, I didn't correct her, even though this time she added even more wild details than before – 'And the dog was jumping up at me and I could see the evil in its eyes, so I pulled Grace onto my back and ran us both right out of there!' – I just went along with the sentiment that I was lucky to be alive and that I owed everything to Kendall.

From my seat in the Booth, I spotted Til over the other side of the canteen. I waved and she looked briefly surprised to see me, but then she came over. She looked awful. Her hair was sticking up at a strange angle and her clothes were all crumpled.

'I didn't know you were back today,' she said.

'Yeah,' I said. 'I am.' Because really, what else was there to say?

She hovered for a moment then she said, 'I'm going to the library to work. You've got a free now, haven't you? You coming?'

I paused. I wanted to ask Til if she was OK, but I knew if I did that in front of other people, she'd just snap that she was fine. 'I'm just going to hang out here for a minute. I'll come and find you in a bit though.'

She nodded, but she didn't say anything and shuffled away. By the time I'd finished answering everyone's excited questions about how much it had hurt and just how big the dog was and if I'd seen a bright light at the end of a tunnel when I was unconscious, it was nearly the end of the period. When I went up to the library, Til was gone.

Later, when Mum came to pick me up from college in the car to save me from getting jostled about on the bus, Til walked past as I climbed into the car.

Mum wound down her window. 'Til! Hello! Do you want a lift?'

Til looked up, surprised to be drawn out of her thoughts. 'Oh no, ta. I'm all right.'

As she walked away across the car park, her coat bunched up around her ears, Mum said, 'Is she OK? She looked awful,' and I explained to Mum about the house and Malcolm and the sleeping in the porch.

'That's terrible,' Mum said. 'She's welcome to stay with us for a few days? You can make her a bed on the floor in your room, can't you?'

I sighed and watched as Til disappeared around the corner and out of sight. I was worried about her but I just didn't know what I could do. And she was never the easiest person to help even when I could think of something useful to suggest. 'But what about her mum and Lady Gaga the dog? We just don't have the room. And I honestly don't think she'd want to anyway.'

Progress So Far

On Friday night, I lay in bed listening to the rain and wind outside my window and looking back over my field notes from the last few weeks. I decide to recap where I was.

<u>**Popularity – Progress so far**</u>
Kendall Cross has on numerous occasions commented that we are friends and that I am special to her

Weekend away with members of the Booth

Average number of messages received over last month: 32 a day – up from 9 a day previously

156 likes received on photo post – highest number to date

Invited to sit in the Booth itself

General level of conversation and interaction up at college – more people know my name, I know more facts about more people.

I sat back and reviewed this summary.

It was good, I knew. It was just such an improvement on how things had been before. It really showed what you could do if you put your mind to something. In a way though, I wanted something official – something to mark how far I'd come. Something to announce my presence on the social scene. Like a debutante ball.

I realised the solution was obvious.

There was something I could do that would solidify my new status as a *someone*, and repair the damage I'd done to Bashed's reputation by ruining the masked ball.

I could throw my own party. For myself. For my birthday.

I could invite everyone I knew and everyone would come and everyone would be there for *me*. Maybe I could do that, and then I could start to wind things down a bit. Because the truth was, I was finding my mission a bit tiring. It was difficult, constantly worrying what other people were making of me, whether I was doing the right thing and being seen in a good light.

I didn't want to just abandon my resolutions and slip back to my life exactly as it was before, but maybe a party, one big event, could be a marker of sorts. I could prove something to myself, that I could be liked, if I wanted to, but then maybe after it was all over I could . . . relax a bit. Stop trying so hard. Get some of my old life back.

I turned to the back of my notebook and began brainstorming ideas, and an hour later I was ready.

I went online and created a new event description:

Roll up! Roll up! Bring your purses to a traditional village fair

Candy-floss stall!

Meat raffle!

Coconut shy!

Homemade lemonade!

A party to celebrate the 17th birthday of Grace Dart

Location: TBC

I hadn't yet worked out exactly where I would hold the fair but with a just a few weeks until my birthday, I had to get the invite up and drawing attention straight away. I also hadn't really worked out the logistics of how I would organise all the stalls and games I had listed, but I had confidence that somehow I would.

With the event description created, my next task was to create the list of guests and I spent the next half an hour searching through my contacts, inviting anyone I thought might even consider attending.

A few minutes later I got a message:

Reeta: A party! Sounds cool, Gracie, I'll be there.

Me: Cool! I've invited loads of people but not sure if any will come

Reeta: Of course they will?? Everyone likes you

Me: I don't feel like many of them even know me that well to be honest

Reeta: That doesn't matter. They know you like them. And that's what's most important to them.

Initially I didn't think much of the message. Reeta was just trying to be reassuring, and I appreciated that.

But, later that evening, as I lay in bed resisting the temptation to check my phone for the fiftieth time to see who had and hadn't accepted my invitation, I couldn't help but go over Reeta's words in my head. Was it true that people only liked me because I liked them? Did they really care about me at all?

In the end I told myself that maybe it didn't matter. I had more friends now than I'd ever had in my life before. Did it really matter *why* they were my friends?

An Actual Witch

Even though my arm was still in a sling, I decided to go back into work on Saturday. I was finding that even your favourite thing in the world (i.e., sitting around the house reading and watching TV on your computer) can get boring if you have too much of it. I reasoned that seeing as my job basically involved sitting in a chair, pressing three buttons on a till and saying 'I don't know, have you googled it' whenever people asked me a question, I would probably be OK to get on with it even though I only had one useable arm.

'Oh, you're back,' Sheila said, looking up from her magazine only briefly when I walked in. 'Jolly good.'

I took my seat behind the till and Sheila decided to position herself and her magazine in front of the feather dusters, which seemed as good a view as any when you're in a hardware shop.

Around mid-morning, the bell rang as the door was opened and I was surprised to see Kendall and Dog walk in.

'Ah!' Kendall screamed when she saw me. 'I forgot you worked here! Look at your little uniform! So cute!'

Kendall noticed Sheila then, still perched on her stall in the corner.

'Oh my god,' she said, gasping suddenly and clutching her chest. 'I thought that was an actual witch sitting there!'

She was whispering but in a loud stage whisper that really was no quieter than her everyday voice.

Sheila didn't look up, but then Sheila doesn't always look up if you address a direct question to her using her name, so that didn't mean she hadn't heard. She reached into her pocket and took out a hardboiled egg. I was used to her snacking throughout the day so didn't think much of it, but as she started to peel away the shell, Kendall stared at her in such open-mouthed horror that you would think Sheila had begun peeling off her own skin.

'Is she going to eat that egg?' Kendall hissed. 'Whole? Here?'

I shrugged.

'That's so weird!' She carried on looking at her in fascination for a while, then she put her hand over her face. 'But the smell! It's like a toilet!'

Kendall started to laugh and Dog stood there smirking, although I don't know how much of the conversation she had heard, seeing as she still had her big headphones on.

'Anyway, catch you later, Gracie,' Kendall said, and they left and I wondered why exactly they'd come in in the first place.

'Your friends,' Sheila called flatly from her corner of the shop, without looking up from her magazine. She didn't say it like a question though, which in a way was good, because I wouldn't have known how to answer it.

Probably Coming

That evening, I began to make headway with the party plans.

I ran through the list of features and attractions I had promised and begun to make a list of what I needed to make them happen.

A candy-floss machine I was sure I could hire, so that wasn't too difficult.

I knew I'd need coconuts for the coconut shy, but how would I go about getting a shy? In fact, what even was a shy?

So far, interest in the village fair party had been good. I had over sixty confirmed attendees. I couldn't truly imagine sixty people coming to a party just for me, but I was pleased nonetheless. I couldn't help but notice, though, that Til hadn't yet responded.

I sent her a message:

Me: Are you coming to my birthday party? It's like a village fair. Should be cool.

Til: Probably.

Me: What does that mean?

**Til: It means probably. I've got other things on my
mind at the moment, it's not exactly my priority**

I didn't know why she had to bite my head off. I didn't
reply.

Although the numbers were looking good online, at college
that week I had several alarming conversations that made
me realise I shouldn't get too confident too soon.

The first one was when I bumped into Martin waiting for
Katie outside one of our lessons and I casually (OK, maybe
not that casually) checked that he really was planning on
coming.

He frowned for a moment, as if the idea of the party was
familiar but he couldn't quite remember the details. 'Uh
yeah. Yeah, I think I said I'd come, didn't I? I'll probably
drop in anyway.'

'What do you mean "probably"?' I said. 'What do you
mean "drop in"? Martin!' I punched him on the arm. 'You
quite specifically clicked the "going" button on the event.
I have you down as a definite!'

'Gracie, Gracie, Gracie,' he said, shaking his head and
grinning. 'No one's a definite at a party. If it was just you
and me doing something, or just you and me and like, two
other people, then I would be a definite. I wouldn't let you
down. But you've got, what, a hundred people signed up?
You've got spares. That means I can relax.'

'What do you mean, spares?'

'Yeah. You know. People to spare. You don't need me. I'm a drop in the ocean. No one is committed when it's a big event. That is Socialising 101. No one worries about letting you down 'cause they figure lots of other people will be there.'

I hadn't heard this theory but that was probably because I didn't throw myself a lot of parties. I realised it did make sense and I'd probably apply the same logic myself if I was just a guest.

Katie came out to join us and I asked her if she was any more committed to coming than Martin.

She was busy trying to push her books back into her bag. 'Yeah . . . probably? When is it again?'

I could hardly believe my ears. How could she say she was coming but not even know when it was? Why couldn't she even remember one date? Here I was, walking around with a notebook full of dates – people's birthdays, parents' anniversaries, the date people got their hamsters – and she couldn't even remember the date of something she herself had promised to do.

'Thirteenth Feb,' I said patiently. Then I added, 'My birthday,' to add a little bit of pressure, because I could see it was needed.

She frowned and looked at her phone. Then she shook her head. 'Ah, no sorry, I can't make that. I'm going away to see my cousins.'

'But . . .' I started, then I stopped because I knew there was no point.

What I wanted to point out was that I'd put in a lot of effort into arranging the party, and that it was important to me, but then I realised that didn't really matter. Not to anyone else. Everyone's own things were important to them. That didn't mean they were important to other people. My big day was just another way to kill a few hours for them that they might or might not drop into depending on if they had a better offer.

I spent the rest of the day feeling despondent and wondering if I should call the whole thing off. On the way home though, a thought occurred to me. It was inspired by what Martin had said:

People felt they were just a drop in the ocean. No one felt they were important enough to the event for it to matter whether they turned up or not. The problem with this attitude though, as I was all too aware, was that if *everyone* didn't turn up because they didn't consider themselves central to proceedings, then I would be left with no one at all. No spares. No guests.

I realised that what I needed to do was to counter this attitude. To show people that they were important. That they mattered. That they were essential to the event and that it made all the difference to me if they attended.

I took out my phone and typed a message.

Getting a bit worried that no one's going to come to this party but then I thought who cares? As long as you come, it'll be good. I'd have a good time with you even if it was just us two!!

I sent the message to everyone who had replied that they were coming to the party, and then to a few more people who hadn't said either way, but who I hoped might be persuaded by the message. I knew that for some of the people, like Very Small Robbie who I had only spoken to once in the dinner queue, it might seem a bit out of the blue, but I hoped they'd be flattered nonetheless.

A few minutes later I started to get replies.

Molly: Aw I'll be there

Martin: Such a flirt, Gracie! OK I'm in.

Reeta: As if I'd miss it for the world!

Very Small Robbie: OK Grace. I will try to come for sure.

By the end of the evening, I'd received over forty messages from people confirming their commitment and telling me not to worry. I knew things could change between now and then, but I felt better.

People felt important. And right now, that was very useful.

Just Us Two

The next day, as I walked across the college car park and down the corridor to my locker, I was greeted – either with a 'hello' or a smile or a wave – by no fewer than eight people. Even though I had been steadily expanding my circle, I had never received such a warm welcome. I could only attribute it to my heartfelt message. Suddenly everyone was feeling important to me and that had clearly made them like me more. Perhaps Reeta was right: people really did just like anyone who liked them.

When I got into the canteen though, the atmosphere changed.

As I went to buy a yoghurt from the vending machine, Kendall called over from the Booth.

'Gracie! Could you come here a moment please? We'd like a word.'

I took my yoghurt from the flap at the bottom of the machine and walked over. They were all looking at me – Kendall, Molly, Jules, Dog, Luke.

'So, I just wanted to read something to you,' Kendall

said, her voice light and breezy. She took out her phone, pressed a few buttons then said, 'Getting a bit worried that no one's going to come to this party but then I thought who cares? As long as you come, it'll be good. I'd have a good time with you even if it was just us two!'

I could feel the heat radiating from my cheeks down my neck and to the tips of my ears. The contents of that message was not meant for a group audience.

Then Kendall turned to Molly. 'Mol, did you get any messages yesterday? From Gracie?'

Molly did a pantomime frown, play-acting thinking about the question. 'You know what, I did! Hold on, let me remember what it said. I *think* it said, "Getting a bit worried that no one's going to come to this party but then I thought who cares? As long as you come, it'll be good. I'd have a good time with you even if it was just us two!"'

'Oh, that's so weird!' Kendall said, refusing to give up her acting, even though she'd made her point. 'That's the same as what I got. Only, I thought it was just for me? Because that's how it sounded, didn't it? "Just us two." Wait – did anyone else get anything like that?'

All the others joined in with the performance, nodding in mock confusion, taking out their phones and pretending to check the details and saying in pretend surprise, 'Oh yeah! I did!' and 'Oh, man, I thought I was the special one!'

Suddenly the act was over and Kendall fixed me with a hard stare. 'Why are you being so fake, Gracie?' she said, shaking her head like a disappointed teacher. 'Not cool. Not cool at all.'

'Listen,' I said, still aware of my bright pink face. 'I can explain. I was just really worried – that bit was true – I was just worried that –'

But Kendall held up her hand to stop me. 'I don't think any of us exactly want to talk to you right now.'

The others shook their heads to signal their agreement. I contemplated pleading my case again, telling them exactly how worried I'd been and how I genuinely did want them all to come, but I could see from their expressions they weren't ready to hear it. In the end I just slunk away and exited the canteen.

When I got to my classroom for my lesson, I opened the page for the event and noticed that already twenty of the confirmed attendees had swapped their response to 'Not going'.

A Crisis

At lunchtime, I found Til and Reeta in the canteen.

'I'm having a crisis,' I said, throwing my bag on the floor, sitting down and putting my head in my hands.

'Join the club,' Til said, pulling up the zip of her hoody to her neck.

'No one's coming to my party,' I told them. 'No one at all.'

'We are,' Reeta said.

'I mean no one import—' I stopped myself. 'I mean, no one else.'

'Well, I don't know what we can do about that,' Reeta said with a helpless shrug. 'I can't be any more than one person at a time.' Then, after thinking about it, she added, 'Unless I bought lots of outfits and then I could arrive in one outfit all like, "Hi, I'm Reeta" and then I could run into the toilet and change into some dungarees and a fake moustache and come back, like –' she lowered her voice to a deep growl – '"Hi, I'm Rupert."'

I just looked at her.

'Or,' she went on. 'I can ask my mum if her friends want

to come. She knows literally ten thousand people. We could fill that room easily.'

I sighed, not sure how I could tell Reeta that her mum's friends weren't exactly my idea of A-listers without offending her. 'Really what I want to do is lure the old guests back. Rather than replace them with new ones.'

'They were all coming before, weren't they?' Reeta said. 'Why did they change their minds?'

'I sent them a nice message,' I said.

Reeta frowned, confused. 'Why wouldn't they like that?'

'Because it was fake,' Til said.

I spun around to look at her. 'It wasn't fake. Why do you always think being nice is fake? Sometimes being nice is just being nice.'

'I don't think being nice is fake. I just think you are. You're fake and you're getting faker by the day with your fake friends you don't even like and who don't like you, and your fake messages and your fake photos online about rescues that didn't even happen. Why are you going around saying Kendall rescued you from the lake? Malcolm said you were out before she even got there. Why do you go along with everything that girl says? It's pathetic.'

Til pushed her chair back roughly, picked up her bag and walked out of the canteen. I thought about going after her, but I didn't know what I would say.

I was angry that she couldn't just let me try to make some new friends, to expand out of our tiny little group of three. But at the same time, I knew I had messed up when it came to the message. It was stupid of me, not to consider that people would talk. That they'd put two and two together.

Something that was really bothering me about the message fiasco was Kendall's reaction to it. And this was because, although my main intention had been to get people interested in my party again, the truth was that as far as Kendall was concerned, everything I'd said in it was real.

In a way, I *would* have liked nothing more than for her to be the only person to turn up to the party, and she and I could have the whole hall to ourselves to spend the evening talking and messing around on the coconut shy and making our own candy-floss. I wanted to try to explain this to her in a way that wasn't too intense but that proved to her I wasn't as fake as she thought.

I hung around her locker at the end of the day, hoping to catch her on her own. When she arrived though, she blanked me, going straight to her locker and fiddling with the code without even acknowledging me.

'Uh, Kendall, can I talk to you?'

She looked up and raised one eyebrow. She seemed unimpressed, but she didn't walk away or actively object to my continuing.

'So listen, and you're not going to believe me, but this is the absolute honest truth. I did send that message to everyone, yes, because I really wanted everyone to feel important and want to come to my party. But really, they're not all important, so you're right, it was fake. But the thing is,' I paused, not sure how to put it without scaring her off. 'You are important. And it is honestly important to me that you come. It's like you said when we were at the house, we could be friends for ever. I know we can.'

She looked at me, her eyes staring straight into mine, and I felt the feeling in my stomach and I thought she was going to pull me into one of her tight hugs and say 'OK Gracie, I knew it was only for me really' or 'Yeah, friends for ever'. But she didn't. Instead she just sighed and said, 'Oh, Grace.'

I felt nervous. 'What?'

'I won't lie, you've been a really good friend to me when I've been going through some tough times. It's been hard with Eddie at university. But I think I've been using you a bit. I'm sorry. I knew you liked me and I was quite enjoying being liked, because Eddie had made me feel quite . . . not liked. But it's not fair on you. Eddie and I are going to make a go of things now. We were talking all last night. And I told him about you and he didn't really like the idea of us spending so much time together now he's my boyfriend again and you clearly have feelings for me. So basically . . . I think we should have some space from each other. It's better for both of us that way.'

I just stared at her. There were a million things I wanted to say: how can you be back with Eddie, when all he ever does is treat you like rubbish? How dare you make out like I've been following you around like a little dog when you're the one who always tells me I'm special? How dare you talk about me with Eddie, who I don't even know?

But in the end I realised there was no point. There was no point in any of it.

I just turned around and walked away.

PART 5:

Where I make a new friend to help an old friend and lose some friends altogether

Everything is Cancelled

As I marched home along the sea-front I decided something:
   I hated Kendall Cross.

Whatever I'd felt for her before, and I still wasn't really
sure what that was, I knew now I hated her with a burning
passion. How had I ever liked her? How had I ever thought
she liked me? I'd broken a bone for her. I'd missed an entire
Christmas. And her only response was call me a disaster
and to get angry at me for messing up a stupid party, and
sending one tiny message she didn't like.

I hoped it all went wrong with her and her horrible
university boyfriend. I hoped he'd message her tonight
and tell her he'd met someone much more glamorous and
attractive and she could feel what it was like to be told you're
special one minute and then told that, actually, sorry, that
was a mistake, you're nothing special at all.

I realised that I was glad that people had started to drop
out of my party. I hoped they all dropped out. I hoped I
never had to see any of them ever again. Why would I want
to spend time with people like them anyway?

Molly, to take one example. She was so boring! All she ever did was look at her phone. And that Dog girl could hardly even be polite to me. And even people like Martin and Katie – they were too wrapped up in each other to care about me.

I didn't want to have a party at all. If a hundred people came, would I be happier, a better person, than if ten came?

No.

And even if a hundred people did come, I knew they wouldn't be coming for me. They'd be coming to see the other ninety-nine people who they liked more than me anyway.

Parties were ridiculous inventions. Why would anyone have one?

Right there and then, on the sea-front with the wind blowing my hair all over my face, I took out my phone and cancelled the event altogether.

It was just as I was pushing my phone back into my pocket and resuming my walk that I heard a voice.

'Grace? It is Grace, isn't it?'

I looked up. It took me a moment to recognise the face, what with the gloom of the winter afternoon and the big scarf she was bundled up in, but she jumped in to remind me.

'Pamela,' she said. 'Pamela Roach. You hosted that lovely retro bingo party for us?'

'Oh,' I said, surprised to find her there, when I'd been in the middle of an angry, in-my-head rant. 'Yes. Hello.'

'How are you, my dear? I heard you had an accident delivering us some masks! I felt ever so bad about that. How are you now? Are you OK?'

And I don't know what came over me, but I began to cry. 'No,' I said, shaking my head. 'Not really.'

What Can I Do?

Twenty minutes later, Pamela and I were in a cosy cafe overlooking the pier, my hands wrapped around a mug of hot chocolate, and I was apologising for the hundredth time for having a minor meltdown in response to a perfectly normal question, and Pamela was telling me for the hundredth time that it didn't matter.

And because after acting so strangely I felt like I owed her an explanation, I told her the whole story: I told her about trying to be popular, about how I'd got into Bashed and how confusing everything was with Kendall.

'And I'm sorry,' I said, 'about your masks party. Because it wasn't just your party I messed up. I've let Mac down too.'

And then I explained about how nice Mac was and about his house burning down and about how I'd tried to raise money for him by making all the masks myself but because of the pond disaster I hadn't been able to give him a penny.

'Well, we can deal with that straight away,' she said, reaching for her handbag. 'Yes, we never got our masks, but you made them and I think that deserves some recompense.' She took out her cheque book and wrote a cheque. She handed it to me. It was for one hundred pounds. 'I've made it out to you, as it's your work I'm paying for, but obviously if you want to donate it to this Mac, then that's up to you.'

'Oh,' I said, looking at the cheque. 'I will. Thank you. I will give it to him. To Mac.'

'I'm afraid the rest of it is all a bit more complicated. That's friendships for you. And matters of the heart. And if you get the two muddled up . . . well.' She just shook her head and gave me a kind smile.

We chatted some more about her children and her work and somewhere in the conversations we got onto who else I was friends with and I ended up telling her about Reeta and Til, and then Til's problem with Lady Gaga and Malcolm and the porch and I said out loud something I'd been trying to bury for a few weeks:

'And I've been a rubbish friend to her. I do know that. She's been having a rough time and I haven't helped at all. I just couldn't see what I could do. So it was easier to focus on my own life.'

But still Pamela didn't tell me off. She just said, 'Sometimes things run away with us. But it's what we do to put them right that matters.'

I nodded. 'Mum says why don't I see if she wants to stay with us, but that's only going to work for a few nights. She doesn't want to be sleeping on my bedroom floor. She needs her own bedroom.'

Pamela stirred her coffee thoughtfully. 'I might have an idea. It might be terrible, but then again, it might not.'

'What?' I said. 'What kind of idea?'

An Offer

One hour later, Pamela and I were standing on the steps to her huge house with the turret in the roof, looking up and down the road.

'There she is!' I said, going to the end of the drive to meet her. 'That's her!'

I wouldn't normally have been so excited at the sight of Til but when I messaged her asking her to meet me I hadn't been totally sure if she'd come.

'What's all this then?' she said, coming to meet me. Pamela had stayed on the doorstep of her house and was watching us with her hands in her coat pockets, and Til looked over to her suspiciously.

'Til, this is Pamela Roach.' I gestured to Pamela that she should come to join us. 'This is her house.'

Til frowned. 'Right. So, not meaning to be rude but, so . . . ?'

Pamela gave Til a warm smile, then she said, 'Why don't you girls have a quick catch-up? I'll be inside.'

'What's going on?' Til asked as soon as Pamela had gone.

'Why are we at this woman's house? Does she really live here? It looks like it's out of a ghost story.'

'I just did some work for her once. But it doesn't really matter where I met her. The point is, she has an offer for you.'

And then I explained the idea that Pamela had put to me in the cafe.

Til stood in the drive of the house staring at me like she wasn't sure if I had lost my mind or if I was setting her up for a practical joke.

'You what?' Til said. 'So you're saying, me and Mum and Lady Gaga, all just pack our bags and move into this house?'

I nodded. 'Yeah, exactly!'

'And she's just going to move out to make way for us? That's the most random thing I've ever heard.'

'It's not though,' I said. 'Not when you think about it. It all makes sense. She says it's way too big for one person, and it is really, but she doesn't want to sell it because she wants her son and his family to live here when they move back. But that won't be for years and you'll have moved out and be doing your own thing by then anyway. So what she wants is to live in a little modern flat where she doesn't have to do anything. But keep this house too. So really, renting this house out is something she's been thinking about for ages.'

Til shook her head. 'Grace, how much do you think that's going to cost? A house that size? We can barely cover the rent on a two-bed flat.'

'I already said all that to her. Honestly. Her main thing is she wants someone looking after it. She doesn't know how to do all the plumbing and fixing like you do, so really you'd be the perfect person. You stop her house falling apart and she lets you live there for really mega cheap.'

Til frowned, but now she seemed more amazed than cross. She stepped back and looked up at the house, her hands in her pockets. 'What's it even like inside? It looks . . . insane.'

'Let's go in,' I said, making for the front door. 'Pamela really wants to show you around.'

Til shrugged. 'OK.'

'And be polite,' I whispered. 'Even if you don't want to take it.'

'I'm always polite', Til muttered but with a small smile, and I realised it was the first time in days I'd seen one of those from her.

When I'd visited the house to host the bingo party, I'd only seen the kitchen and the lounge, but as Pamela gave us a guided tour, I realised there was so much more to it. There were two upper floors, both with three bedrooms, although most of them were completely empty at the moment so could have been used for anything. At the very top there was a huge attic room, completely empty except for a sofa by the window with a lamp at its side.

'If you go over to that window, it's got quite a nice view.'

Til crossed the room and looked out. 'Wow,' she said. 'You can see the whole town.'

'I hardly ever come up here now,' Pamela said with a sigh. 'It really is the most ridiculous waste.'

In all the rooms Pamela seemed to take on the role of a kind of Jekyll and Hyde estate agent. She'd start by pointing out the good features – 'All the rooms have got little sinks in the corner, it can be quite useful really' – but then she'd feel the need to be honest about the drawbacks – 'but of course at least half of them aren't working. I have no idea why'. Each time she pointed out a problem or something that needed fixing, Til would offer a solution or her theory on what the issue could be, and Pamela would say 'Yes. Yes, that's a thought' and nod seriously.

When we were out in the garden Pamela had pointed out the woods at the end and said, 'We always wanted a wooded area, for the children to play in. It is nice to wander around in, of an afternoon.' She turned to Til and said, 'So I'm not trying to pretend it's a palace, Lord knows there are bits falling off it left, right and centre, but it is spacious. And I would so appreciate someone with some practical skills being around to tackle things. You don't need to say now, of course you'll need to speak with your mother, but do you think it could work for you?'

Til nodded and ran her hand through her hair. 'Yeah. Yeah, absolutely. But it's just . . .' She shook her head.

'What?' I asked her. 'Come on, Til, it'd be way better than Malcolm's porch, wouldn't it?'

'No. Yeah. It's not that. The house is great, but . . . it's just Lady Gaga. I know the place is perfect and I know Mum will see she hasn't got any choice but to re-home her because it really is too good an opportunity to turn down, but it's going to be –'

'Oh, didn't you tell her?' Pamela said, cutting her off and turning to me.

'No, sorry, I forgot.'

Til looked round at me.

'It's all fine, about Lady Gaga,' I said. 'Sorry, I should have said. I told Pamela about her right from the beginning. She's totally allowed.'

Til frowned, bemused. 'You really want a massive bear-dog in your lush house? Has Grace told you how big she is? She's not a little spaniel or anything. This is fifty-five kilos of pure dog energy.'

'Oh, I know!' Pamela said. 'Grace has shown me what a beautiful dog she is. She is quite welcome here, I can assure you. How lovely to imagine her bounding around the woods there! But I do wonder, if I might ask one small favour.'

'We won't let her upstairs,' Til said. 'We can just keep her to the kitchen if you like.'

'Oh no, not that,' Pamela said with a wave of her hand. 'Let her sleep on the beds if you like. Give her her own bedroom! It's just, the thing is, I have always so loved dogs, ever since I was a girl, but I've never been able to have one as an adult, because first my husband had the most intense phobia and then my son was allergic. And of course I shan't be able to have one in this little flat I've got my eye on, but I wondered if I might borrow yours, as it were, from time to time? Come by and pick Lady Gaga up, take her to the park and throw a few balls for her? Would that be too much of an imposition?'

Til laughed. 'Seriously? Nope. That would not be an imposition at all. Be my guest. Be my absolute guest.'

A New Event

Although I was pleased to be able to hand over the one hundred pounds Pamela had given me to Mac, and he made such a big deal of thanking me and saying how it made such a difference to him you would think he would be able to buy an entire castle with it, I still felt bad. My messing up the masked ball – and deciding not to have anything else to do with Bashed – meant that there wouldn't be any more where that had come from. And that, once again, I'd made him a promise I couldn't keep.

So, after much discussion with Reeta, two days after cancelling my birthday party, I set up a new event page:

Auction of dreams – things money can't buy (only it can, on this occasion, so bring your money)

I kept things vague in the post, mostly because I was still fine-tuning the details, but I let people know it would help Mac, and I spoke to my tutor, Piers, who confirmed I could use the college hall for free. This time, I didn't invite people personally or require an RSVP. I made it a public event and made it clear that people should pass it on to anyone who they thought might be interested. This time, I told Reeta to let her mum's ten thousand friends know they were more than welcome.

The day after I set up the event, I was doing some work for college at my desk, when I heard my phone buzzing. When I looked at the screen, I saw Kendall was calling me.

I sat there with the phone in my hand, weighing up what to do. On the one hand I was still angry with her. She had made me feel like a total idiot and I'd realised that, in a way, I *was* a total idiot. But even though I knew it was better, for now at least, that I had nothing at all to do with her, there was a part of me that still found the sight of her name on my phone screen just a tiny bit exciting.

In the end, I put my phone on silent, chucked it on my bed and waited for her to give up.

A little while later though, I got a message:

Kendall: Please call me back. I know you're mad with me and don't want to be friends any more but this isn't about that. It's about the auction.

So, just out of curiosity, I did ring her. And actually, I was quite glad I did.

The Auction of Dreams

Two weeks later, Til, Reeta and I were in the college hall, setting out chairs for the auction. Most of the effort – gathering the auction lots – had already been done, so there wasn't much to do to get the room ready, but still, I felt nervous.

'What if no one comes?' I said.

'Oh my god, what if you ask that question one more time and I actually kill you?' Til said, but she was smiling.

'Everyone's coming, Gracie,' Reeta said. 'Like, almost literally everyone I have ever heard of. It's going to be amazing.'

I didn't think it was going to be amazing. I didn't need it to be amazing. I just needed it to work. I needed people to come. I didn't need them to come to make me feel popular or that I'd had a good idea, I just needed them to come and bid and to be able to give Mac something that would help him get his home back together. I couldn't let him down again.

At six forty-five, Til and I took our position at the drinks stand, and Reeta opened the doors to let the bidders in. It was a slow trickle at first, but by seven o'clock, there was standing room only in the hall.

Martin, who I had managed to persuade to play the part of auctioneer for the night, took to the stage. I hadn't given him any particular clothing instructions, but I was interested to see he believed that the perfect uniform to lead an auction was black dungarees, a pink shirt and a bow tie.

'Thank you, everyone, for coming!' he said into the microphone. 'As you know we're all here for our good friend Mac. He said he didn't want to come tonight and put pressure on everyone to put their hands in their pockets and bid high, but in his absence, let me just say . . . put your hands in your pockets and bid high!' Everyone laughed and Martin grinned down at them all, then he said, 'So without further ado, let's get started with lot number one, something I'm sure each and every one of us could make use of: an entire afternoon of free plumbing services, ably carried out by our good friend Til Romero!'

Martin gestured to Til and everyone clapped and cheered, and she smiled and did a kind of pretend salute. Out of the corner of her mouth she muttered to me, 'I told him to say basic jobs only. I'm still training.'

'You can work out the details later,' I whispered back, just as one of Reeta's mum's colleagues shouted out, 'Forty pounds!'

We'd received so many donations of goods and services to offer as lots, that as each item sold, we had to move quickly onto the next. I was pleased to see that the atmosphere of excitement was translating into lively bidding and everything was selling for much more than I'd hoped.

Katie Boyd's sister paid £200 for a personal fitness plan, created by Reeta.

A boy from the year above won a sailing day with my dad with a bid for £130.

Mrs Palmer from the accounts office paid £95 for a week of dog walks supplied by Pamela Roach.

I think Til would have bid for that one herself, had it not been for the fact Pamela was already walking Lady Gaga three or four times a week completely free.

In fact, the only lot that didn't sell – or, in fact, get any bids at all – was a waxing session with Reeta.

'Sorry, Reets,' I said, when Martin declared it unsold.

'Oh no, it's fine,' she said. 'I'm pleased. Because between you and me, Gracie, I haven't the first idea how to do a wax. I was just making it up as I went along for you!'

'Wonderful,' I said. 'I would never have guessed.'

By nine o'clock, nearly all the lots had been sold and we'd raised £2,300 for Mac, which was much more than I'd expected.

But we had one more lot.

'OK. So the last lot of the night,' Martin called out, 'is great news for anyone with a celebration coming up. A full party service from Bashed Limited, who can offer you everything you need to make your party go with a swing. That includes a cake in any shape, style, colour or flavour you choose, a full buffet to whatever theme you like, and three hours of absolute first-class entertainment. Any party you like! Give your kids a birthday party they won't forget! Give your grandad the cabaret he's always wanted!'

'Martin!' I hissed from my position next to the stage.

He shot me a grin. 'OK, no cabarets, but all sorts of other fun on offer. Honestly, folks, this is a once in a lifetime opportunity – because Bashed are closing down after this. This is their grand finale and it could be all yours!'

It was when I'd called Kendall back that she'd told me that she was shutting Bashed down.

'Why?' I said. 'I thought you loved it.'

'I did, in a way, but also in a way, I was doing it to impress Eddie. To show him I could do it. And in a way, I've done that. But in another way, I don't care what he thinks any more.'

'It is over between you then?'

'Yeah. For good this time. No more calls. No more "I miss you". *Over* over. Over and out.'

'OK,' I said. 'So . . . sorry, but I don't get what this has to do with the auction?'

'Well, you know how we kept some money, in the business, for investment and supplies and stuff?'

'Yeah.' I remembered the wodge of cash I'd seen in her drawer.

'Well, there's a bit left. Like, maybe fifty quid or something. And I was going to say to you, you can give it to Mac. But then I thought, if I spent it on ingredients, we could offer a cake or food – or both – for the auction. And that way, we could turn the fifty pounds into . . . more than fifty pounds.'

I thought about this for a moment. I had to admit it made sense. So I'd agreed to not only accept her donation, but to join her, one last time, to make sure the lot raised as much money as possible by providing whatever they needed to make it a full party offering. And she'd agreed that for once she'd make a cake that looked like the ones on the website.

'So, let's start the bidding for the party of your dreams at a hundred pounds!'

The bids flew in and by the time Martin shouted 'Sold, to the lady in the spotty jumper!' they had reached £600.

The lady in the spotty jumper I recognised as the mum of one of Paddy's friends from nursery, and in addition to little Reuben I knew she also had a pair of six-year-old twins, so there was a very good chance Bashed's last event was to be a very lively children's party. Still, it might be fun, I told myself. And it was the last one, after all.

'So that's it!' Martin shouted. 'That's your lot, so to speak. And I'm pleased to announce we've made a grand total of . . . £2,900 . . . for Mac! Now, as I say, Mac couldn't be with us tonight, but I know for certain that –'

'Oh, hi, hello,' a voice from the back of the room said, and everyone swivelled round in their chairs to see where it had come from.

'I take it back!' Martin said. 'Because here he is, the man of the moment! The Macster! Macky McIntosh! Macaroni Chee – OK, I'll stop. Do you want to come up, Mac? The mic's all yours.'

Mac made his way to the stage and stood there for a moment, just grinning around at everyone. 'Well, what can I say! I mean, wow, really, that's all. Just wow! Everyone at the college has been amazing since the fire but this is the absolute icing on the doughnut. So I just want to say a huge, massive thank-you. To Grace and Til and Reeta and Martin for organising this and to everyone who donated the amazing prizes and to everyone who bid on them. It's like I was saying to Mrs Mac just now, if I could go back and change history so the fire didn't happen, would I? Do you know, I'm not sure I would, because if there'd been no fire then I would never have known just how lovely all you people are.'

Everyone started to clap then and Mac made his way off the stage and down to the back of the hall, and as he did so, everyone on the end of a row held out their hands for him to high-five them as he went past, like he was a tennis player leaving the court after a brilliant win.

When the auction was over and everyone was wrapping themselves up ready to head back into the winter night, Til and I began stacking the chairs and putting them back where they belonged at the back of the stage.

'Went pretty well then,' Til said, carrying two chairs in each hand.

'Yeah.' I took them from her and added them to the stack. 'It did actually, didn't it? Better than I expected, really.'

'Was quite surprised Kendall donated something though. Didn't have her down as the type of person to put herself out to help people.'

I had never properly explained to Til why I had suddenly stopped spending time with Kendall or officially acknowledged that I was mistaken to have looked up to her so much, but I knew that Til knew something had happened.

'She sounded sad,' I said. 'On the phone.'

Til didn't say anything, she just continued stacking the chairs in silence.

It had occurred to me, after the call, that I'd been miserable because I'd felt she'd treated me like an idiot and she was miserable because she thought Eddie had treated her like an idiot. I wondered if anyone was making Eddie miserable by treating him like an idiot. Maybe it was all just a chain, everyone upset with someone, and treating someone else badly because they were miserable.

'I know Kendall's not the greatest person ever,' I said eventually. 'I know I got carried away thinking she was, I dunno . . . something special. I think she's probably not a bad person either though.'

Til stood on the edge of the stage with her hands on her hips, surveying which chairs still needed to be rounded up. 'She's probably just a person, really. Good and bad. Neither. Both.' She shrugged. 'I dunno.'

'Me neither,' I said.

I went and stood next to her. She turned to look at me. 'So is that it then? Are you popular now? Mission accomplished?'

I rolled my eyes. 'Mission aborted.'

'Mission aborted after partial success?' Til suggested, which was probably one of the most generous things she'd ever said to me.

I laughed. 'Maybe. I'm done with trying to recruit numbers. But I still want some people to like me!'

Til raised an eyebrow. 'Some people? Anyone in particular?'

'Yeah. Stop trying to make me say it! You know I want you to like me again and not be angry with me any more.'

Til made a face. 'Oh, I'm so over it. I'm really not into sulking. That's more your thing.'

I decided to let that comment pass, just this once.

'How's it going in the haunted house? Lady Gaga enjoying herself?'

Til nodded. 'She is, she is. We all are. It's insane to have so much space. Me and Mum have been getting on better than we have ever in my whole life. Seriously. We're like this weird little happy family of three.'

'Well, that's good?'

Til nodded. 'Yeah. It really is.'

'If we were the type,' I said, 'we'd probably hug now.'

Til weighed this up. 'Yeah. We probably would.' We continued standing there on the edge of the stage, making no movement towards each other because if there is one thing we were agreed on, it's that we were really not the type to hug.

However, there was one person who did not subscribe to our code.

'Oh! Wait! Are we hugging!' came Reeta's excited voice as she burst through the stage curtains. 'Not without me, we're not! Wait for me! Group hug!' And she launched herself at both of us, bundling us together, her arms around our necks like we were in a three-way wrestling match and she was very much winning. 'I love you guys!' she said into our ears. 'I love it when we're all friends again!'

Jess Vallance

Jess Vallance works as a freelance writer and lives near Brighton. Her YA novels for Hot Key Books are *Birdy* and *The Yellow Room*, as well as the Gracie Dart novels, *You Only Live Once* and *To Be Perfectly Honest*.

Follow Jess at www.jessvallance.com or on Twitter: @JessVallance1

Thank you for choosing a Hot Key book.

If you want to know more about our authors and what we publish, you can find us online.

You can start at our website

www.hotkeybooks.com

And you can also find us on:

We hope to see you soon!